Anton Chekhov
An Anonymous Story

I

THROUGH causes which it is not the time to go into in detail, I had to enter the service of a Petersburg official called Orlov, in the capacity of a footman. He was about five and thirty, and was called Georgy* Ivanitch.

*Both g's hard, as in "Gorgon"; e like ai in rain.

I entered this Orlov's service on account of his father, a prominent political man, whom I looked upon as a serious enemy of my cause. I reckoned that, living with the son, I should -- from the conversations I should hear, and from the letters and papers I should find on the table -- learn every detail of the father's plans and intentions.

As a rule at eleven o'clock in the morning the electric bell rang in my footman's quarters to let me know that my master was awake. When I went into the bedroom with his polished shoes and brushed clothes, Georgy Ivanitch would be sitting in his bed with a face that looked, not drowsy, but rather exhausted by sleep, and he would gaze off in one direction without any sign of satisfaction at having waked. I helped him to dress, and he let me do it with an air of reluctance without speaking or noticing my presence; then with his head wet with washing, smelling of fresh scent, he used to go into the dining-room to drink his coffee. He used to sit at the table, sipping his coffee and glancing through the newspapers, while the maid Polya and I stood respectfully at the door gazing at him. Two grown-up persons had to stand watching with the gravest attention a third drinking coffee and munching rusks. It was probably ludicrous and grotesque, but I saw nothing humiliating in having to stand near the door, though I was quite as well born and well educated as Orlov himself.

I was in the first stage of consumption, and was suffering from something else, possibly even more serious than consumption. I don't know whether it was the effect of my illness or of an incipient change in my philosophy of life of which I was not conscious at the time, but I was, day by day, more possessed by a passionate,

---

4

irritating longing for ordinary everyday life. I yearned for mental tranquillity, health, fresh air, good food. I was becoming a dreamer, and, like a dreamer, I did not know exactly what I wanted. Sometimes I felt inclined to go into a monastery, to sit there for days together by the window and gaze at the trees and the fields; sometimes I fancied I would buy fifteen acres of land and settle down as a country gentleman; sometimes I inwardly vowed to take up science and become a professor at some provincial university. I was a retired navy lieutenant; I dreamed of the sea, of our squadron, and of the corvette in which I had made the cruise round the world. I longed to experience again the indescribable feeling when, walking in the tropical forest or looking at the sunset in the Bay of Bengal, one is thrilled with ecstasy and at the same time homesick. I dreamed of mountains, women, music, and, with the curiosity of a child, I looked into people's faces, listened to their voices. And when I stood at the door and watched Orlov sipping his coffee, I felt not a footman, but a man interested in everything in the world, even in Orlov.

In appearance Orlov was a typical Petersburger, with narrow shoulders, a long waist, sunken temples, eyes of an indefinite colour, and scanty, dingy-coloured hair, beard and moustaches. His face had a stale, unpleasant look, though it was studiously cared for. It was particularly unpleasant when he was asleep or lost in thought. It is not worth while describing a quite ordinary appearance; besides, Petersburg is not Spain, and a man's appearance is not of much consequence even in love affairs, and is only of value to a handsome footman or coachman. I have spoken of Orlov's face and hair only because there was something in his appearance worth mentioning. When Orlov took a newspaper or book, whatever it might be, or met people, whoever they be, an ironical smile began to come into his eyes, and his whole countenance assumed an expression of light mockery in which there was no malice. Before reading or hearing anything he always had his irony in readiness, as a savage has his shield. It was an habitual irony, like some old liquor brewed years ago, and now it came into his face probably without any participation of his will, as it were by reflex action. But of that later.

Soon after midday he took his portfolio, full of papers, and drove to his office. He dined away from home and returned after eight

—

5

o'clock. I used to light the lamp and candles in his study, and he would sit down in a low chair with his legs stretched out on another chair, and, reclining in that position, would begin reading. Almost every day he brought in new books with him or received parcels of them from the shops, and there were heaps of books in three languages, to say nothing of Russian, which he had read and thrown away, in the corners of my room and under my bed. He read with extraordinary rapidity. They say: "Tell me what you read, and I'll tell you who you are." That may be true, but it was absolutely impossible to judge of Orlov by what he read. It was a regular hotchpotch. Philosophy, French novels, political economy, finance, new poets, and publications of the firm Posrednik* -- and he read it all with the same rapidity and with the same ironical expression in his eyes.

* I.e., Tchertkov and others, publishers of Tolstoy, who issued good literature for peasants' reading.

After ten o'clock he carefully dressed, often in evening dress, very rarely in his kammer-junker's uniform, and went out, returning in the morning.

Our relations were quiet and peaceful, and we never had any misunderstanding. As a rule he did not notice my presence, and when he talked to me there was no expression of irony on his face -- he evidently did not look upon me as a human being.

I only once saw him angry. One day -- it was a week after I had entered his service -- he came back from some dinner at nine o'clock; his face looked ill-humoured and exhausted. When I followed him into his study to light the candles, he said to me:

"There's a nasty smell in the flat."

"No, the air is fresh," I answered.

"I tell you, there's a bad smell," he answered irritably.

"I open the movable panes every day."

"Don't argue, blockhead!" he shouted.

I was offended, and was on the point of answering, and goodness knows how it would have ended if Polya, who knew her master better than I did, had not intervened.

"There really is a disagreeable smell," she said, raising her eyebrows. "What can it be from? Stepan, open the pane in the drawing-room, and light the fire."

With much bustle and many exclamations, she went through all the rooms, rustling her skirts and squeezing the sprayer with a hissing sound. And Orlov was still out of humour; he was obviously restraining himself not to vent his ill-temper aloud. He was sitting at the table and rapidly writing a letter. After writing a few lines he snorted angrily and tore it up, then he began writing again.

"Damn them all!" he muttered. "They expect me to have an abnormal memory!"

At last the letter was written; he got up from the table and said, turning to me:

"Go to Znamensky Street and deliver this letter to Zinaida Fyodorovna Krasnovsky in person. But first ask the porter whether her husband -- that is, Mr. Krasnovsky -- has returned yet. If he has returned, don't deliver the letter, but come back. Wait a minute! . . . If she asks whether I have any one here, tell her that there have been two gentlemen here since eight o'clock, writing something."

I drove to Znamensky Street. The porter told me that Mr. Krasnovsky had not yet come in, and I made my way up to the third storey. The door was opened by a tall, stout, drab-coloured flunkey with black whiskers, who in a sleepy, churlish, and apathetic voice, such as only flunkeys use in addressing other flunkeys, asked me what I wanted. Before I had time to answer, a lady dressed in black came hurriedly into the hall. She screwed up her eyes and looked at me.

"Is Zinaida Fyodorovna at home?" I asked.

"That is me," said the lady.

"A letter from Georgy Ivanitch."

She tore the letter open impatiently, and holding it in both hands, so that I saw her sparkling diamond rings, she began reading. I made out a pale face with soft lines, a prominent chin, and long dark lashes. From her appearance I should not have judged the lady to be more than five and twenty.

"Give him my thanks and my greetings," she said when she had finished the letter. "Is there any one with Georgy Ivanitch?" she asked softly, joyfully, and as though ashamed of her mistrust.

"Two gentlemen," I answered. "They're writing something."

"Give him my greetings and thanks," she repeated, bending her head sideways, and, reading the letter as she walked, she went noiselessly out. I saw few women at that time, and this lady of whom I had a passing glimpse made an impression on me. As I walked home I recalled her face and the delicate fragrance about her, and fell to dreaming. By the time I got home Orlov had gone out.

II

And so my relations with my employer were quiet and peaceful, but still the unclean and degrading element which I so dreaded on becoming a footman was conspicuous and made itself felt every day. I did not get on with Polya. She was a well-fed and pampered hussy who adored Orlov because he was a gentleman and despised me because I was a footman. Probably, from the point of view of a real flunkey or cook, she was fascinating, with her red cheeks, her turned-up nose, her coquettish glances, and the plumpness, one might almost say fatness, of her person. She powdered her face, coloured her lips and eyebrows, laced herself in, and wore a bustle, and a bangle made of coins. She walked with little ripping steps; as she walked she swayed, or, as they say, wriggled her shoulders and back. The rustle of her skirts, the creaking of her stays, the jingle her bangle and the vulgar smell of lip salve, toilet vinegar, and scent

---

8

stolen from her master, aroused me whilst I was doing the rooms with her in the morning a sensation as though I were taking part with her in some abomination.

Either because I did not steal as she did, or because I displayed no desire to become her lover, which she probably looked upon as an insult, or perhaps because she felt that I was a man of a different order, she hated me from the first day. My inexperience, my appearance -- so unlike a flunkey -- and my illness, seemed to her pitiful and excited her disgust. I had a bad cough at that time, and sometimes at night I prevented her from sleeping, as our rooms were only divided by a wooden partition, and every morning she said to me:

"Again you didn't let me sleep. You ought to be in hospital instead of in service."

She so genuinely believed that I was hardly a human being, but something infinitely below her, that, like the Roman matrons who were not ashamed to bathe before their slaves, she sometimes went about in my presence in nothing but her chemise.

Once when I was in a happy, dreamy mood, I asked her at dinner (we had soup and roast meat sent in from a restaurant every day)

"Polya, do you believe in God?"

"Why, of course!"

"Then," I went on, "you believe there will be a day of judgment, and that we shall have to answer to God for every evil action?"

She gave me no reply, but simply made a contemptuous grimace, and, looking that time at her cold eyes and over-fed expression, I realised that for her complete and finished personality no God, no conscience, no laws existed, and that if I had had to set fire to the house, to murder or to rob, I could not have hired a better accomplice.

—

In my novel surroundings I felt very uncomfortable for the first week at Orlov's before I got used to being addressed as "thou," and being constantly obliged to tell lies (saying "My master is not at home" when he was). In my flunkey's swallow-tail I felt as though I were in armour. But I grew accustomed to it in time. Like a genuine footman, I waited at table, tidied the rooms, ran and drove about on errands of all sorts. When Orlov did not want to keep an appointment with Zinaida Fyodorovna, or when he forgot that he had promised to go and see her, I drove to Znamensky Street, put a letter into her hands and told a lie. And the result of it all was quite different from what I had expected when I became a footman. Every day of this new life of mine was wasted for me and my cause, as Orlov never spoke of his father, nor did his visitors, and all I could learn of the stateman's doings was, as before, what I could glean from the newspapers or from correspondence with my comrades. The hundreds of notes and papers I used to find in the study and read had not the remotest connection with what I was looking for. Orlov was absolutely uninterested in his father's political work, and looked as though he had never heard of it, or as though his father had long been dead.

III

Every Thursday we had visitors.

I ordered a piece of roast beef from the restaurant and telephoned to Eliseyev's to send us caviare, cheese, oysters, and so on. I bought playing-cards. Polya was busy all day getting ready the tea-things and the dinner service. To tell the truth, this spurt of activity came as a pleasant change in our idle life, and Thursdays were for us the most interesting days.

Only three visitors used to come. The most important and perhaps the most interesting was the one called Pekarsky -- a tall, lean man of five and forty, with a long hooked nose, with a big black beard, and a bald patch on his head. His eyes were large and prominent, and his expression was grave and thoughtful like that of a Greek philosopher. He was on the board of management of some railway, and also had some post in a bank; he was a consulting lawyer in some important Government institution, and had business relations with a large number of private persons as a trustee, chairman of committees, and so on. He was of quite a low grade in the service, and modestly spoke of himself as a lawyer, but he had a vast influence. A note or card from him was enough to make a celebrated doctor, a director of a railway, or a great dignitary see any one without waiting; and it was said that through his protection one might obtain even a post of the Fourth Class, and get any sort of unpleasant business hushed up. He was looked upon as a very intelligent man, but his was a strange, peculiar intelligence. He was able to multiply 213 by 373 in his head instantaneously, or turn English pounds into German marks without help of pencil or paper; he understood finance and railway business thoroughly, and the machinery of Russian administration had no secrets for him; he was a most skilful pleader in civil suits, and it was not easy to get the better of him at law. But that exceptional intelligence could not grasp many things which are understood even by some stupid people. For instance, he was absolutely unable to understand why people are depressed, why they weep, shoot themselves, and even kill others; why they fret about things that do not affect them personally, and why they laugh when they read Gogol or Shtchedrin. . . . Everything abstract, everything belonging to the domain of thought and feeling, was to him boring and incomprehensible, like music to one who has no ear. He looked at people simply from the business point of view, and divided them into competent and incompetent. No other classification existed for him. Honesty and rectitude were only signs of competence. Drinking, gambling, and debauchery were permissible, but must not be allowed to interfere with business. Believing in God was rather stupid, but religion ought be safeguarded, as the common people must have some principle to restrain them, otherwise they would not work. Punishment is only necessary as deterrent. There was no need to go away for holidays, as it was just as nice in town. And so on. He was a widower and had no children, but lived on a large scale, as though he had a family, and paid thousand roubles a year for his flat.

The second visitor, Kukushkin, an actual civil councillor though a young man, was short, and was conspicuous for his extremely unpleasant appearance, which was due to the disproportion between his fat, puffy body and his lean little face. His lips were puckered up suavely, and his little trimmed moustaches looked as though they had been fixed on with glue. He was a man with the manners of a lizard. He did not walk, but, as it were, crept along with tiny steps, squirming and sniggering, and when he laughed he showed his teeth. He was a clerk on special commissions, and did nothing, though he received a good salary, especially in the summer, when special and lucrative jobs were found for him. He was a man of personal ambition, not only to the marrow of his bones, but more fundamentally -- to the last drop of his blood; but even in his ambitions he was petty and did not rely on himself, but was building his career on the chance favour flung him by his superiors. For the sake of obtaining some foreign decoration, or for the sake of having his name mentioned in the newspapers as having been present at some special service in the company of other great personages, he was ready to submit to any kind of humiliation, to beg, to flatter, to promise. He flattered Orlov and Pekarsky from cowardice, because he thought they were powerful; he flattered Polya and me because we were in the service of a powerful man. Whenever I took off his fur coat he tittered and asked me: "Stepan, are you married?" and then unseemly vulgarities followed -- by way of showing me special attention. Kukushkin flattered Orlov's weaknesses, humoured his corrupted and blasé ways; to please him he affected malicious raillery and atheism, in his company criticised persons before whom in other places he would slavishly grovel. When at supper they talked of love and women, he pretended to be a subtle and perverse voluptuary. As a rule, one may say, Petersburg rakes are fond of talking of their abnormal tastes. Some young actual civil councillor is perfectly satisfied with the embraces of his cook or of some unhappy street-walker on the Nevsky Prospect, but to listen to him you would think he was contaminated by all the vices of East and West combined, that he was an honourary member of a dozen iniquitous secret societies and was already marked by the police. Kukushkin lied about himself in an unconscionable way, and they did not exactly disbelieve him, but paid little heed to his incredible stories.

The third guest was Gruzin, the son of a worthy and learned general; a man of Orlov's age, with long hair, short-sighted eyes, and gold spectacles. I remember his long white fingers, that looked like a pianist's; and, indeed, there was something of a musician, of a

---

12

virtuoso, about his whole figure. The first violins in orchestras look just like that. He used to cough, suffered from migraine, and seemed invalidish and delicate. Probably at home he was dressed and undressed like a baby. He had finished at the College of Jurisprudence, and had at first served in the Department of Justice, then he was transferred to the Senate; he left that, and through patronage had received a post in the Department of Crown Estates, and had soon afterwards given that up. In my time he was serving in Orlov's department; he was his head-clerk, but he said that he should soon exchange into the Department of Justice again. He took his duties and his shifting about from one post to another with exceptional levity, and when people talked before him seriously of grades in the service, decorations, salaries, he smiled good-naturedly and repeated Prutkov's aphorism: "It's only in the Government service you learn the truth." He had a little wife with a wrinkled face, who was very jealous of him, and five weedy-looking children. He was unfaithful to his wife, he was only fond of his children when he saw them, and on the whole was rather indifferent to his family, and made fun of them. He and his family existed on credit, borrowing wherever they could at every opportunity, even from his superiors in the office and porters in people's houses. His was a flabby nature; he was so lazy that he did not care what became of himself, and drifted along heedless where or why he was going. He went where he was taken. If he was taken to some low haunt, he went; if wine was set before him, he drank -- if it were not put before him, he abstained; if wives were abused in his presence, he abused his wife, declaring she had ruined his life -- when wives were praised, he praised his and said quite sincerely: "I am very fond of her, poor thing!" He had no fur coat and always wore a rug which smelt of the nursery. When at supper he rolled balls of bread and drank a great deal of red wine, absorbed in thought, strange to say, I used to feel almost certain that there was something in him of which perhaps he had a vague sense, though in the bustle and vulgarity of his daily life he had not time to understand and appreciate it. He played a little on the piano. Sometimes he would sit down at the piano, play a chord or two, and begin singing softly:

"What does the coming day bring to me?"
But at once, as though afraid, he would get up and walk from the piano.

The visitors usually arrived about ten o'clock. They played cards in Orlov's study, and Polya and I handed them tea. It was only on these occasions that I could gauge the full sweetness of a flunkey's life. Standing for four or five hours at the door, watching that no one's glass should be empty, changing the ash-trays, running to the table to pick up the chalk or a card when it was dropped, and, above all, standing, waiting, being attentive without venturing to speak, to cough, to smile -- is harder, I assure you, is harder than the hardest of field labour. I have stood on watch at sea for four hours at a stretch on stormy winter nights, and to my thinking it is an infinitely easier duty.

They used to play cards till two, sometimes till three o'clock at night, and then, stretching, they would go into the dining-room to supper, or, as Orlov said, for a snack of something. At supper there was conversation. It usually began by Orlov's speaking with laughing eyes of some acquaintance, of some book he had lately been reading, of a new appointment or Government scheme. Kukushkin, always ingratiating, would fall into his tone, and what followed was to me, in my mood at that time, a revolting exhibition. The irony of Orlov and his friends knew no bounds, and spared no one and nothing. If they spoke of religion, it was with irony; they spoke of philosophy, of the significance and object of life -- irony again, if any one began about the peasantry, it was with irony.

There is in Petersburg a species of men whose specialty it is to jeer at every aspect of life; they cannot even pass by a starving man or a suicide without saying something vulgar. But Orlov and his friends did not jeer or make jokes, they talked ironically. They used to say that there was no God, and personality was completely lost at death; the immortals only existed in the French Academy. Real good did not and could not possibly exist, as its existence was conditional upon human perfection, which was a logical absurdity. Russia was a country as poor and dull as Persia. The intellectual class was hopeless; in Pekarsky's opinion the overwhelming majority in it were incompetent persons, good for nothing. The people were drunken,

14

lazy, thievish, and degenerate. We had no science, our literature was uncouth, our commerce rested on swindling -- "No selling without cheating." And everything was in that style, and everything was a subject for laughter.

Towards the end of supper the wine made them more good-humoured, and they passed to more lively conversation. They laughed over Gruzin's family life, over Kukushkin's conquests, or at Pekarsky, who had, they said, in his account book one page headed Charity and another Physiological Necessities. They said that no wife was faithful; that there was no wife from whom one could not, with practice, obtain caresses without leaving her drawing-room while her husband was sitting in his study close by; that girls in their teens were perverted and knew everything. Orlov had preserved a letter of a schoolgirl of fourteen: on her way home from school she had "hooked an officer on the Nevsky," who had, it appears, taken her home with him, and had only let her go late in the evening; and she hastened to write about this to her school friend to share her joy with her. They maintained that there was not and never had been such a thing as moral purity, and that evidently it was unnecessary; mankind had so far done very well without it. The harm done by so-called vice was undoubtedly exaggerated. Vices which are punished by our legal code had not prevented Diogenes from being a philosopher and a teacher. Cæsar and Cicero were profligates and at the same time great men. Cato in his old age married a young girl, and yet he was regarded as a great ascetic and a pillar of morality.

At three or four o'clock the party broke up or they went off together out of town, or to Officers' Street, to the house of a certain Varvara Ossipovna, while I retired to my quarters, and was kept awake a long while by coughing and headache.

IV

Three weeks after I entered Orlov's service -- it was Sunday morning, I remember -- somebody rang the bell. It was not yet eleven, and Orlov was still asleep. I went to open the door. You can imagine my astonishment when I found a lady in a veil standing at the door on the landing.

"Is Georgy Ivanitch up?" she asked.

From her voice I recognised Zinaida Fyodorovna, to whom I had taken letters in Znamensky Street. I don't remember whether I had time or self-possession to answer her -- I was taken aback at seeing her. And, indeed, she did not need my answer. In a flash she had darted by me, and, filling the hall with the fragrance of her perfume, which I remember to this day, she went on, and her footsteps died away. For at least half an hour afterwards I heard nothing. But again some one rang. This time it was a smartly dressed girl, who looked like a maid in a wealthy family, accompanied by our house porter. Both were out of breath, carrying two trunks and a dress-basket.

"These are for Zinaida Fyodorovna," said the girl.

And she went down without saying another word. All this was mysterious, and made Polya, who had a deep admiration for the pranks of her betters, smile slyly to herself; she looked as though she would like to say, "So that's what we're up to," and she walked about the whole time on tiptoe. At last we heard footsteps; Zinaida Fyodorovna came quickly into the hall, and seeing me at the door of my room, said:

"Stepan, take Georgy Ivanitch his things."

When I went in to Orlov with his clothes and his boots, he was sitting on the bed with his feet on the bearskin rug. There was an air of embarrassment about his whole figure. He did not notice me, and my menial opinion did not interest him; he was evidently perturbed and embarrassed before himself, before his inner eye. He dressed, washed, and used his combs and brushes silently and deliberately, as though allowing himself time to think over his position and to

---

16

reflect, and even from his back one could see he was troubled and dissatisfied with himself.

They drank coffee together. Zinaida Fyodorovna poured out coffee for herself and for Orlov, then she put her elbows on the table and laughed.

"I still can't believe it," she said. "When one has been a long while on one's travels and reaches a hotel at last, it's difficult to believe that one hasn't to go on. It is pleasant to breathe freely."

With the expression of a child who very much wants to be mischievous, she sighed with relief and laughed again.

"You will excuse me," said Orlov, nodding towards the coffee. "Reading at breakfast is a habit I can't get over. But I can do two things at once -- read and listen."

"Read away. . . . You shall keep your habits and your freedom. But why do you look so solemn? Are you always like that in the morning, or is it only to-day? Aren't you glad?"

"Yes, I am. But I must own I am a little overwhelmed."

"Why? You had plenty of time to prepare yourself for my descent upon you. I've been threatening to come every day."

"Yes, but I didn't expect you to carry out your threat to-day."

"I didn't expect it myself, but that's all the better. It's all the better, my dear. It's best to have an aching tooth out and have done with it."

"Yes, of course."

"Oh, my dear," she said, closing her eyes, "all is well that ends well; but before this happy ending, what suffering there has been! My laughing means nothing; I am glad, I am happy, but I feel more like crying than laughing. Yesterday I had to fight a regular battle," she went on in French. "God alone knows how wretched I was. But I

———

17

laugh because I can't believe in it. I keep fancying that my sitting here drinking coffee with you is not real, but a dream."

Then, still speaking French, she described how she had broken with her husband the day before and her eyes were alternately full of tears and of laughter while she gazed with rapture at Orlov. She told him her husband had long suspected her, but had avoided explanations; they had frequent quarrels, and usually at the most heated moment he would suddenly subside into silence and depart to his study for fear that in his exasperation he might give utterance to his suspicions or she might herself begin to speak openly. And she had felt guilty, worthless, incapable of taking a bold and serious step, and that had made her hate herself and her husband more every day, and she had suffered the torments of hell. But the day before, when during a quarrel he had cried out in a tearful voice, "My God, when will it end?" and had walked off to his study, she had run after him like a cat after a mouse, and, preventing him from shutting the door, she had cried that she hated him with her whole soul. Then he let her come into the study and she had told him everything, had confessed that she loved some one else, that that some one else was her real, most lawful husband, and that she thought it her true duty to go away to him that very day, whatever might happen, if she were to be shot for it.

"There's a very romantic streak in you," Orlov interrupted, keeping his eyes fixed on the newspaper.

She laughed and went on talking without touching her coffee. Her cheeks glowed and she was a little embarrassed by it, and she looked in confusion at Polya and me. From what she went on to say I learnt that her husband had answered her with threats, reproaches, and finally tears, and that it would have been more accurate to say that she, and not he, had been the attacking party.

"Yes, my dear, so long as I was worked up, everything went all right," she told Orlov; "but as night came on, my spirits sank. You don't believe in God, George, but I do believe a little, and I fear retribution. God requires of us patience, magnanimity, self-sacrifice, and here I am refusing to be patient and want to remodel my life to suit myself. Is that right? What if from the point of view of God it's

18

wrong? At two o'clock in the night my husband came to me and said: 'You dare not go away. I'll fetch you back through the police and make a scandal.' And soon afterwards I saw him like a shadow at my door. 'Have mercy on me! Your elopement may injure me in the service. Those words had a coarse effect upon me and made me feel stiff all over. I felt as though the retribution were beginning already; I began crying and trembling with terror. I felt as though the ceiling would fall upon me, that I should be dragged off to the police-station at once, that you would grow cold to me -- all sorts of things, in fact! I thought I would go into a nunnery or become a nurse, and give up all thought of happiness, but then I remembered that you loved me, and that I had no right to dispose of myself without your knowledge; and everything in my mind was in a tangle -- I was in despair and did not know what to do or think. But the sun rose and I grew happier. As soon as it was morning I dashed off to you. Ah, what I've been through, dear one! I haven't slept for two nights!

She was tired out and excited. She was sleepy, and at the same time she wanted to talk endlessly, to laugh and to cry, and to go to a restaurant to lunch that she might feel her freedom.

"You have a cosy flat, but I am afraid it may be small for the two of us," she said, walking rapidly through all the rooms when they had finished breakfast. "What room will you give me? I like this one because it is next to your study."

At one o'clock she changed her dress in the room next to the study, which from that time she called hers, and she went off with Orlov to lunch. They dined, too, at a restaurant, and spent the long interval between lunch and dinner in shopping. Till late at night I was opening the door to messengers and errand-boys from the shops. They bought, among other things, a splendid pier-glass, a dressing-table, a bedstead, and a gorgeous tea service which we did not need. They bought a regular collection of copper saucepans, which we set in a row on the shelf in our cold, empty kitchen. As we were unpacking the tea service Polya's eyes gleamed, and she looked at me two or three times with hatred and fear that I, not she, would be the first to steal one of these charming cups. A lady's writing-table, very expensive and inconvenient, came too. It was evident that

---

19

Zinaida Fyodorovna contemplated settling with us for good, and meant to make the flat her home.

She came back with Orlov between nine and ten. Full of proud consciousness that she had done something bold and out of the common, passionately in love, and, as she imagined, passionately loved, exhausted, looking forward to a sweet sound sleep, Zinaida Fyodorovna was revelling in her new life. She squeezed her hands together in the excess of her joy, declared that everything was delightful, and swore that she would love Orlov for ever; and these vows, and the naïve, almost childish confidence that she too was deeply loved and would be loved forever, made her at least five years younger. She talked charming nonsense and laughed at herself.

"There's no other blessing greater than freedom!" she said, forcing herself to say something serious and edifying. "How absurd it is when you think of it! We attach no value to our own opinion even when it is wise, but tremble before the opinion of all sorts of stupid people. Up to the last minute I was afraid of what other people would say, but as soon as I followed my own instinct and made up my mind to go my own way, my eyes were opened, I overcame my silly fears, and now I am happy and wish every one could be as happy!"

But her thoughts immediately took another turn, and she began talking of another flat, of wallpapers, horses, a trip to Switzerland and Italy. Orlov was tired by the restaurants and the shops, and was still suffering from the same uneasiness that I had noticed in the morning. He smiled, but more from politeness than pleasure, and when she spoke of anything seriously, he agreed ironically: "Oh, yes."

"Stepan, make haste and find us a good cook," she said to me.

"There's no need to be in a hurry over the kitchen arrangements," said Orlov, looking at me coldly. "We must first move into another flat."

20

We had never had cooking done at home nor kept horses, because, as he said, "he did not like disorder about him," and only put up with having Polya and me in his flat from necessity. The so-called domestic hearth with its everyday joys and its petty cares offended his taste as vulgarity; to be with child, or to have children and talk about them, was bad form, like a petty bourgeois. And I began to feel very curious to see how these two creatures would get on together in one flat -- she, domestic and home-loving with her copper saucepans and her dreams of a good cook and horses; and he, fond of saying to his friends that a decent and orderly man's flat ought, like a warship, to have nothing in it superfluous -- no women, no children, no rags, no kitchen utensils.

V

Then I will tell you what happened the following Thursday. That day Zinaida Fyodorovna dined at Content's or Donon's. Orlov returned home alone, and Zinaida Fyodorovna, as I learnt afterwards, went to the Petersburg Side to spend with her old governess the time visitors were with us. Orlov did not care to show her to his friends. I realised that at breakfast, when he began assuring her that for the sake of her peace of mind it was essential to give up his Thursday evenings.

As usual the visitors arrived at almost the same time.

"Is your mistress at home, too?" Kukushkin asked me in a whisper.

"No, sir," I answered.

He went in with a sly, oily look in his eyes, smiling mysteriously, rubbing his hands, which were cold from the frost.

"I have the honour to congratulate you," he said to Orlov, shaking all over with ingratiating, obsequious laughter. "May you increase and multiply like the cedars of Lebanon."

The visitors went into the bedroom, and were extremely jocose on the subject of a pair of feminine slippers, the rug that had been put down between the two beds, and a grey dressing-jacket that hung at the foot of the bedstead. They were amused that the obstinate man who despised all the common place details of love had been caught in feminine snares in such a simple and ordinary way.

"He who pointed the finger of scorn is bowing the knee in homage," Kukushkin repeated several times. He had, I may say in parenthesis, an unpleasant habit of adorning his conversation with texts in Church Slavonic. "Sh-sh!" he said as they went from the bedroom into the room next to the study. "Sh-sh! Here Gretchen is dreaming of her Faust."

He went off into a peal of laughter as though he had said something very amusing. I watched Gruzin, expecting that his musical soul would not endure this laughter, but I was mistaken. His thin, good-natured face beamed with pleasure. When they sat down to play cards, he, lisping and choking with laughter, said that all that "dear George" wanted to complete his domestic felicity was a cherry-wood pipe and a guitar. Pekarsky laughed sedately, but from his serious expression one could see that Orlov's new love affair was distasteful to him. He did not understand what had happened exactly.

"But how about the husband?" he asked in perplexity, after they had played three rubbers.

"I don't know," answered Orlov.

Pekarsky combed his big beard with his fingers and sank into thought, and he did not speak again till supper-time. When they were seated at supper, he began deliberately, drawling every word:

"Altogether, excuse my saying so, I don't understand either of you. You might love each other and break the seventh commandment to your heart's content -- that I understand. Yes, that's comprehensible. But why make the husband a party to your secrets? Was there any need for that?"

"But does it make any difference?"

"Hm! . . . ." Pekarsky mused. "Well, then, let me tell you this, my friend," he went on, evidently thinking hard: "if I ever marry again and you take it into your head to seduce my wife, please do it so that I don't notice it. It's much more honest to deceive a man than to break up his family life and injure his reputation. I understand. You both imagine that in living together openly you are doing something exceptionally honourable and advanced, but I can't agree with that . . . what shall I call it? . . . . romantic attitude?"

Orlov made no reply. He was out of humour and disinclined to talk. Pekarsky, still perplexed, drummed on the table with his fingers, thought a little, and said:

"I don't understand you, all the same. You are not a student and she is not a dressmaker. You are both of you people with means. I should have thought you might have arranged a separate flat for her."

"No, I couldn't. Read Turgenev."

"Why should I read him? I have read him already."

"Turgenev teaches us in his novels that every exalted, noble-minded girl should follow the man she loves to the ends of the earth, and should serve his idea," said Orlov, screwing up his eyes ironically. "The ends of the earth are poetic license; the earth and all its ends can be reduced to the flat of the man she loves. . . . And so not to live in the same flat with the woman who loves you is to deny her her exalted vocation and to refuse to share her ideals. Yes, my dear fellow, Turgenev wrote, and I have to suffer for it."

"What Turgenev has got to do with it I don't understand," said Gruzin softly, and he shrugged his shoulders. "Do you remember, George, how in 'Three Meetings' he is walking late in the evening somewhere in Italy, and suddenly hears, 'Vieni pensando a me segretamente,'" Gruzin hummed. "It's fine."

But she hasn't come to settle with you by force," said Pekarsky. "It was your own wish."

23

"What next! Far from wishing it, I never imagined that this would ever happen. When she said she was coming to live with me, I thought it was a charming joke on her part."

Everybody laughed.

"I couldn't have wished for such a thing," said Orlov in the tone of a man compelled to justify himself. "I am not a Turgenev hero, and if I ever wanted to free Bulgaria I shouldn't need a lady's company. I look upon love primarily as a necessity of my physical nature, degrading and antagonistic to my spirit; it must either be satisfied with discretion or renounced altogether, otherwise it will bring into one's life elements as unclean as itself. For it to be an enjoyment and not a torment, I will try to make it beautiful and to surround it with a mass of illusions. I should never go and see a woman unless I were sure beforehand that she would be beautiful and fascinating; and I should never go unless I were in the mood. And it is only in that way that we succeed in deceiving one another, and fancying that we are in love and happy. But can I wish for copper saucepans and untidy hair, or like to be seen myself when I am unwashed or out of humour? Zinaida Fyodorovna in the simplicity of her heart wants me to love what I have been shunning all my life. She wants my flat to smell of cooking and washing up; she wants all the fuss of moving into another flat, of driving about with her own horses; she wants to count over my linen and to look after my health; she wants to meddle in my personal life at every instant, and to watch over every step; and at the same time she assures me genuinely that my habits and my freedom will be untouched. She is persuaded that, like a young couple, we shall very soon go for a honeymoon -- that is, she wants to be with me all the time in trains and hotels, while I like to read on the journey and cannot endure talking in trains."

"You should give her a talking to," said Pekarsky.

"What! Do you suppose she would understand me? Why, we think so differently. In her opinion, to leave one's papa and mamma or one's husband for the sake of the man one loves is the height of civic virtue, while I look upon it as childish. To fall in love and run away with a man to her means beginning a new life, while to my mind it means nothing at all. Love and man constitute the chief interest of her life, and possibly it is the philosophy of the unconscious at work in her. Try and make her believe that love is only a simple physical need, like the need of food or clothes; that it doesn't mean the end of the world if wives and husbands are unsatisfactory; that a man may be a profligate and a libertine, and yet a man of honour and a genius; and that, on the other hand, one may abstain from the pleasures of love and at the same time be a stupid, vicious animal! The civilised man of to-day, even among the lower classes -- for instance, the French workman -- spends ten sous on dinner, five sous on his wine, and five or ten sous on woman, and devotes his brain and nerves entirely to his work. But Zinaida Fyodorovna assigns to love not so many sous, but her whole soul. I might give her a talking to, but she would raise a wail in answer, and declare in all sincerity that I had ruined her, that she had nothing left to live for."

"Don't say anything to her," said Pekarsky, "but simply take a separate flat for her, that's all."

"That's easy to say."

There was a brief silence.

"But she is charming," said Kukushkin. "She is exquisite. Such women imagine that they will be in love for ever, and abandon themselves with tragic intensity."

"But one must keep a head on one's shoulders," said Orlov; "one must be reasonable. All experience gained from everyday life and handed down in innumerable novels and plays, uniformly confirms the fact that adultery and cohabitation of any sort between decent people never lasts longer than two or at most three years, however great the love may have been at the beginning. That she ought to know. And so all this business of moving, of saucepans, hopes of eternal love and harmony, are nothing but a desire to delude herself and me. She is charming and exquisite -- who denies it? But she has turned my life upside down; what I have regarded as trivial and nonsensical till now she has forced me to raise to the level of a serious problem; I serve an idol whom I have never looked upon as God. She is charming -- exquisite, but for some reason now when I am going home, I feel uneasy, as though I expected to meet with something inconvenient at home, such as workmen pulling the stove to pieces and blocking up the place with heaps of bricks. In fact, I am no longer giving up to love a sous, but part of my peace of mind and my nerves. And that's bad."

"And she doesn't hear this villain!" sighed Kukushkin. "My dear sir," he said theatrically, "I will relieve you from the burdensome obligation to love that adorable creature! I will wrest Zinaida Fyodorovna from you!"

"You may . . ." said Orlov carelessly.

For half a minute Kukushkin laughed a shrill little laugh, shaking all over, then he said:

"Look out; I am in earnest! Don't you play the Othello afterwards!"

They all began talking of Kukushkin's indefatigable energy in love affairs, how irresistible he was to women, and what a danger he was to husbands; and how the devil would roast him in the other world for his immorality in this. He screwed up his eyes and remained silent, and when the names of ladies of their acquaintance were mentioned, he held up his little finger -- as though to say they mustn't give away other people's secrets.

Orlov suddenly looked at his watch.

His friends understood, and began to take their leave. I remember that Gruzin, who was a little drunk, was wearisomely long in getting off. He put on his coat, which was cut like children's coats in poor families, pulled up the collar, and began telling some long-winded story; then, seeing he was not listened to, he flung the rug that smelt of the nursery over one shoulder, and with a guilty and imploring face begged me to find his hat.

"George, my angel," he said tenderly. "Do as I ask you, dear boy; come out of town with us!"

"You can go, but I can't. I am in the position of a married man now."

"She is a dear, she won't be angry. My dear chief, come along! It's glorious weather; there's snow and frost. . . . Upon my word, you want shaking up a bit; you are out of humour. I don't know what the devil is the matter with you. . . ."

Orlov stretched, yawned, and looked at Pekarsky.

"Are you going?" he said, hesitating.

"I don't know. Perhaps."

"Shall I get drunk? All right, I'll come," said Orlov after some hesitation. "Wait a minute; I'll get some money."

He went into the study, and Gruzin slouched in, too, dragging his rug after him. A minute later both came back into the hall. Gruzin, a little drunk and very pleased, was crumpling a ten-rouble note in his hands.

"We'll settle up to-morrow," he said. "And she is kind, she won't be cross. . . . She is my Lisotchka's godmother; I am fond of her, poor thing! Ah, my dear fellow!" he laughed joyfully, and pressing his forehead on Pekarsky's back. "Ah, Pekarsky, my dear soul! Advocatissimus -- as dry as a biscuit, but you bet he is fond of women. . . ."

"Fat ones," said Orlov, putting on his fur coat. "But let us get off, or we shall be meeting her on the doorstep."

"'Vieni pensando a me segretamente,'" hummed Gruzin.

At last they drove off: Orlov did not sleep at home, and returned next day at dinner-time.

VI

Zinaida Fyodorovna had lost her gold watch, a present from her father. This loss surprised and alarmed her. She spent half a day going through the rooms, looking helplessly on all the tables and on all the windows. But the watch had disappeared completely.

Only three days afterwards Zinaida Fyodorovna, on coming in, left her purse in the hall. Luckily for me, on that occasion it was not I but Polya who helped her off with her coat. When the purse was missed, it could not be found in the hall.

"Strange," said Zinaida Fyodorovna in bewilderment. "I distinctly remember taking it out of my pocket to pay the cabman . . . and then I put it here near the looking-glass. It's very odd!"

I had not stolen it, but I felt as though I had stolen it and had been caught in the theft. Tears actually came into my eyes. When they were seated at dinner, Zinaida Fyodorovna said to Orlov in French:

"There seem to be spirits in the flat. I lost my purse in the hall to-day, and now, lo and behold, it is on my table. But it's not quite a disinterested trick of the spirits. They took out a gold coin and twenty roubles in notes."

"You are always losing something; first it's your watch and then it's your money . . ." said Orlov. "Why is it nothing of the sort ever happens to me?"

A minute later Zinaida Fyodorovna had forgotten the trick played by the spirits, and was telling with a laugh how the week before she had ordered some notepaper and had forgotten to give her new address, and the shop had sent the paper to her old home at her husband's, who had to pay twelve roubles for it. And suddenly she turned her eyes on Polya and looked at her intently. She blushed as she did so, and was so confused that she began talking of something else.

When I took in the coffee to the study, Orlov was standing with his back to the fire and she was sitting in an arm-chair facing him.

"I am not in a bad temper at all," she was saying in French. "But I have been putting things together, and now I see it clearly. I can give you the day and the hour when she stole my watch. And the purse? There can be no doubt about it. Oh!" she laughed as she took the coffee from me. "Now I understand why I am always losing my handkerchiefs and gloves. Whatever you say, I shall dismiss the magpie to-morrow and send Stepan for my Sofya. She is not a thief and has not got such a repulsive appearance."

"You are out of humour. To-morrow you will feel differently, and will realise that you can't discharge people simply because you suspect them."

"It's not suspicion; it's certainty," said Zinaida Fyodorovna. "So long as I suspected that unhappy-faced, poor-looking valet of yours, I said nothing. It's too bad of you not to believe me, George."

"If we think differently about anything, it doesn't follow that I don't believe you. You may be right," said Orlov, turning round and flinging his cigarette-end into the fire, "but there is no need to be excited about it, anyway. In fact, I must say, I never expected my humble establishment would cause you so much serious worry and agitation. You've lost a gold coin: never mind -- you may have a hundred of mine; but to change my habits, to pick up a new housemaid, to wait till she is used to the place -- all that's a tedious, tiring business and does not suit me. Our present maid certainly is fat, and has, perhaps, a weakness for gloves and handkerchiefs, but she is perfectly well behaved, well trained, and does not shriek when Kukushkin pinches her."

"You mean that you can't part with her? . . . Why don't you say so?"

"Are you jealous?"

"Yes, I am," said Zinaida Fyodorovna, decidedly.

"Thank you."

"Yes, I am jealous," she repeated, and tears glistened in her eyes. "No, it's something worse . . . which I find it difficult to find a name

---

29

for." She pressed her hands on her temples, and went on impulsively. "You men are so disgusting! It's horrible!"

"I see nothing horrible about it."

"I've not seen it; I don't know; but they say that you men begin with housemaids as boys, and get so used to it that you feel no repugnance. I don't know, I don't know, but I have actually read . . .George, of course you are right," she said, going up to Orlov and changing to a caressing and imploring tone. "I really am out of humour to-day. But, you must understand, I can't help it. She disgusts me and I am afraid of her. It makes me miserable to see her."

"Surely you can rise above such paltriness?" said Orlov, shrugging his shoulders in perplexity, and walking away from the fire. "Nothing could be simpler: take no notice of her, and then she won't disgust you, and you won't need to make a regular tragedy out of a trifle."

I went out of the study, and I don't know what answer Orlov received. Whatever it was, Polya remained. After that Zinaida Fyodorovna never applied to her for anything, and evidently tried to dispense with her services. When Polya handed her anything or even passed by her, jingling her bangle and rustling her skirts, she shuddered.

I believe that if Gruzin or Pekarsky had asked Orlov to dismiss Polya he would have done so without the slightest hesitation, without troubling about any explanations. He was easily persuaded, like all indifferent people. But in his relations with Zinaida Fyodorovna he displayed for some reason, even in trifles, an obstinacy which sometimes was almost irrational. I knew beforehand that if Zinaida Fyodorovna liked anything, it would be certain not to please Orlov. When on coming in from shopping she made haste to show him with pride some new purchase, he would glance at it and say coldly that the more unnecessary objects they had in the flat, the less airy it would be. It sometimes happened that after putting on his dress clothes to go out somewhere, and after saying good-bye to Zinaida Fyodorovna, he would suddenly change his mind and remain at

---

home from sheer perversity. I used to think that he remained at home then simply in order to feel injured.

"Why are you staying?" said Zinaida Fyodorovna, with a show of vexation, though at the same time she was radiant with delight. "Why do you? You are not accustomed to spending your evenings at home, and I don't want you to alter your habits on my account. Do go out as usual, if you don't want me to feel guilty."

"No one is blaming you," said Orlov.

With the air of a victim he stretched himself in his easy-chair in the study, and shading his eyes with his hand, took up a book. But soon the book dropped from his hand, he turned heavily in his chair, and again screened his eyes as though from the sun. Now he felt annoyed that he had not gone out.

"May I come in?" Zinaida Fyodorovna would say, coming irresolutely into the study. "Are you reading? I felt dull by myself, and have come just for a minute . . . to have a peep at you."

I remember one evening she went in like that, irresolutely and inappropriately, and sank on the rug at Orlov's feet, and from her soft, timid movements one could see that she did not understand his mood and was afraid.

"You are always reading . . ." she said cajolingly, evidently wishing to flatter him. "Do you know, George, what is one of the secrets of your success? You are very clever and well-read. What book have you there?"

Orlov answered. A silence followed for some minutes which seemed to me very long. I was standing in the drawing-room, from which I could watch them, and was afraid of coughing.

"There is something I wanted to tell you," said Zinaida Fyodorovna, and she laughed; "shall I? Very likely you'll laugh and say that I flatter myself. You know I want, I want horribly to believe that you are staying at home to-night for my sake . . . that we might spend the evening together. Yes? May I think so?"

31

"Do," he said, screening his eyes. "The really happy man is he who thinks not only of what is, but of what is not."

"That was a long sentence which I did not quite understand. You mean happy people live in their imagination. Yes, that's true. I love to sit in your study in the evening and let my thoughts carry me far, far away. . . . It's pleasant sometimes to dream. Let us dream aloud, George."

"I've never been at a girls' boarding-school; I never learnt the art."

"You are out of humour?" said Zinaida Fyodorovna, taking Orlov's hand. "Tell me why. When you are like that, I'm afraid. I don't know whether your head aches or whether you are angry with me. . . ."

Again there was a silence lasting several long minutes.

"Why have you changed?" she said softly. "Why are you never so tender or so gay as you used to be at Znamensky Street? I've been with you almost a month, but it seems to me as though we had not yet begun to live, and have not yet talked of anything as we ought to. You always answer me with jokes or else with a long cold lecture like a teacher. And there is something cold in your jokes. . . . Why have you given up talking to me seriously?"

"I always talk seriously."

"Well, then, let us talk. For God's sake, George. . . . Shall we?"

"Certainly, but about what?"

"Let us talk of our life, of our future," said Zinaida Fyodorovna dreamily. "I keep making plans for our life, plans and plans -- and I enjoy doing it so! George, I'll begin with the question, when are you going to give up your post?"

"What for?" asked Orlov, taking his hand from his forehead.

"With your views you cannot remain in the service. You are out of place there."

"My views?" Orlov repeated. "My views? In conviction and temperament I am an ordinary official, one of Shtchedrin's heroes. You take me for something different, I venture to assure you."

"Joking again, George!"

"Not in the least. The service does not satisfy me, perhaps; but, anyway, it is better for me than anything else. I am used to it, and in it I meet men of my own sort; I am in my place there and find it tolerable."

"You hate the service and it revolts you."

"Indeed? If I resign my post, take to dreaming aloud and letting myself be carried away into another world, do you suppose that that world would be less hateful to me than the service?"

"You are ready to libel yourself in order to contradict me." Zinaida Fyodorovna was offended and got up. "I am sorry I began this talk."

"Why are you angry? I am not angry with you for not being an official. Every one lives as he likes best."

"Why, do you live as you like best? Are you free? To spend your life writing documents that are opposed to your own ideas," Zinaida Fyodorovna went on, clasping her hands in despair: "to submit to authority, congratulate your superiors at the New Year, and then cards and nothing but cards: worst of all, to be working for a system which must be distasteful to you -- no, George, no! You should not make such horrid jokes. It's dreadful. You are a man of ideas, and you ought to be working for your ideas and nothing else."

"You really take me for quite a different person from what I am," sighed Orlov.

"Say simply that you don't want to talk to me. You dislike me, that's all," said Zinaida Fyodorovna through her tears.

"Look here, my dear," said Orlov admonishingly, sitting up in his chair. "You were pleased to observe yourself that I am a clever, well-read man, and to teach one who knows does nothing but harm. I know very well all the ideas, great and small, which you mean when you call me a man of ideas. So if I prefer the service and cards to those ideas, you may be sure I have good grounds for it. That's one thing. Secondly, you have, so far as I know, never been in the service, and can only have drawn your ideas of Government service from anecdotes and indifferent novels. So it would not be amiss for us to make a compact, once for all, not to talk of things we know already or of things about which we are not competent to speak."

"Why do you speak to me like that?" said Zinaida Fyodorovna, stepping back as though in horror. "What for? George, for God's sake, think what you are saying!"

Her voice quivered and broke; she was evidently trying to restrain her tears, but she suddenly broke into sobs.

"George, my darling, I am perishing!" she said in French, dropping down before Orlov, and laying her head on his knees. "I am miserable, I am exhausted. I can't bear it, I can't bear it. . . . In my childhood my hateful, depraved stepmother, then my husband, now you . . . you! . . . You meet my mad love with coldness and irony. . . . And that horrible, insolent servant," she went on, sobbing. "Yes, yes, I see: I am not your wife nor your friend, but a woman you don't respect because she has become your mistress. . . . I shall kill myself!"

I had not expected that her words and her tears would make such an impression on Orlov. He flushed, moved uneasily in his chair, and instead of irony, his face wore a look of stupid, schoolboyish dismay.

"My darling, you misunderstood me," he muttered helplessly, touching her hair and her shoulders. "Forgive me, I entreat you. I was unjust and I hate myself."

"I insult you with my whining and complaints. You are a true, generous . . . rare man -- I am conscious of it every minute; but I've been horribly depressed for the last few days. . ."

Zinaida Fyodorovna impulsively embraced Orlov and kissed him on the cheek.

"Only please don't cry," he said.

"No, no. . . . I've had my cry, and now I am better."

"As for the servant, she shall be gone to-morrow," he said, still moving uneasily in his chair.

"No, she must stay, George! Do you hear? I am not afraid of her now. . . . One must rise above trifles and not imagine silly things. You are right! You are a wonderful, rare person!"

She soon left off crying. With tears glistening on her eyelashes, sitting on Orlov's knee, she told him in a low voice something touching, something like a reminiscence of childhood and youth. She stroked his face, kissed him, and carefully examined his hands with the rings on them and the charms on his watch-chain. She was carried away by what she was saying, and by being near the man she loved, and probably because her tears had cleared and refreshed her soul, there was a note of wonderful candour and sincerity in her voice. And Orlov played with her chestnut hair and kissed her hands, noiselessly pressing them to his lips.

Then they had tea in the study, and Zinaida Fyodorovna read aloud some letters. Soon after midnight they went to bed. I had a fearful pain in my side that night, and I not get warm or go to sleep till morning. I could hear Orlov go from the bedroom into his study. After sitting there about an hour, he rang the bell. In my pain and exhaustion I forgot all the rules and conventions, and went to his study in my night attire, barefooted. Orlov, in his dressing-gown and cap, was standing in the doorway, waiting for me.

"When you are sent for you should come dressed," he said sternly. "Bring some fresh candles."

I was about to apologise, but suddenly broke into a violent cough, and clutched at the side of the door to save myself from falling.

"Are you ill?" said Orlov.

I believe it was the first time of our acquaintance that he addressed me not in the singular -- goodness knows why. Most likely, in my night clothes and with my face distorted by coughing, I played my part poorly, and was very little like a flunkey.

"If you are ill, why do you take a place?" he said.

"That I may not die of starvation," I answered.

"How disgusting it all is, really!" he said softly, going up to his table.

While hurriedly getting into my coat, I put up and lighted fresh candles. He was sitting at the table, with feet stretched out on a low chair, cutting a book.

I left him deeply engrossed, and the book did not drop out of his hands as it had done in the evening.

VII

Now that I am writing these lines I am restrained by that dread of appearing sentimental and ridiculous, in which I have been trained from childhood; when I want to be affectionate or to say anything tender, I don't know how to be natural. And it is that dread, together with lack of practice, that prevents me from being able to express with perfect clearness what was passing in my soul at that time.

I was not in love with Zinaida Fyodorovna, but in the ordinary human feeling I had for her, there was far more youth, freshness, and joyousness than in Orlov's love.

As I worked in the morning, cleaning boots or sweeping the rooms, I waited with a thrill at my heart for the moment when I should hear her voice and her footsteps. To stand watching her as she drank her coffee in the morning or ate her lunch, to hold her fur coat for her in the hall, and to put the goloshes on her little feet while she rested her hand on my shoulder; then to wait till the hall porter rang up for me, to meet her at the door, cold, and rosy, powdered with the snow, to listen to her brief exclamations about the frost or the cabman -- if only you knew how much all that meant to me! I longed to be in love, to have a wife and child of my own. I wanted my future wife to have just such a face, such a voice. I dreamed of it at dinner, and in the street when I was sent on some errand, and when I lay awake at night. Orlov rejected with disgust children, cooking, copper saucepans, and feminine knicknacks and I gathered them all up, tenderly cherished them in my dreams, loved them, and begged them of destiny. I had visions of a wife, a nursery, a little house with garden paths. . . .

I knew that if I did love her I could never dare hope for the miracle of her returning my love, but that reflection did not worry me. In my quiet, modest feeling akin to ordinary affection, there was no jealousy of Orlov or even envy of him, since I realised that for a wreck like me happiness was only to be found in dreams.

When Zinaida Fyodorovna sat up night after night for her George, looking immovably at a book of which she never turned a page, or when she shuddered and turned pale at Polya's crossing the room, I suffered with her, and the idea occurred to me to lance this festering wound as quickly as possible by letting her know what was said here at supper on Thursdays; but -- how was it to be done? More and more often I saw her tears. For the first weeks she laughed and sang to herself, even when Orlov was not at home, but by the second month there was a mournful stillness in our flat broken only on Thursday evenings.

She flattered Orlov, and to wring from him a counterfeit smile or kiss, was ready to go on her knees to him, to fawn on him like a dog. Even when her heart was heaviest, she could not resist glancing into a looking-glass if she passed one and straightening her hair. It seemed strange to me that she could still take an interest in clothes and go into ecstasies over her purchases. It did not seem in keeping with her genuine grief. She paid attention to the fashions and ordered expensive dresses. What for? On whose account? I particularly remember one dress which cost four hundred roubles. To give four hundred roubles for an unnecessary, useless dress while women for their hard day's work get only twenty kopecks a day without food, and the makers of Venice and Brussels lace are only paid half a franc a day on the supposition that they can earn the rest by immorality! And it seemed strange to me that Zinaida Fyodorovna was not conscious of it; it vexed me. But she had only to go out of the house for me to find excuses and explanations for everything, and to be waiting eagerly for the hall porter to ring for me.

She treated me as a flunkey, a being of a lower order. One may pat a dog, and yet not notice it; I was given orders and asked questions, but my presence was not observed. My master and mistress thought it unseemly to say more to me than is usually said to servants; if when waiting at dinner I had laughed or put in my word in the conversation, they would certainly have thought I was mad and have dismissed me. Zinaida Fyodorovna was favourably disposed to me, all the same. When she was sending me on some errand or explaining to me the working of a new lamp or anything of that sort, her face was extraordinarily kind, frank, and cordial, and her eyes looked me straight in the face. At such moments I always fancied she remembered with gratitude how I used to bring her letters to Znamensky Street. When she rang the bell, Polya, who considered me her favourite and hated me for it, used to say with a jeering smile:

"Go along, your mistress wants you."

Zinaida Fyodorovna considered me as a being of a lower order, and did not suspect that if any one in the house were in a humiliating position it was she. She did not know that I, a footman, was unhappy on her account, and used to ask myself twenty times a day what was in store for her and how it would all end. Things were growing visibly worse day by day. After the evening on which they had talked of his official work, Orlov, who could not endure tears, unmistakably began to avoid conversation with her; whenever Zinaida Fyodorovna began to argue, or to beseech him, or seemed on the point of crying, he seized some plausible excuse for retreating to his study or going out. He more and more rarely slept at home, and still more rarely dined there: on Thursdays he was the one to suggest some expedition to his friends. Zinaida Fyodorovna was still dreaming of having the cooking done at home, of moving to a new flat, of travelling abroad, but her dreams remained dreams. Dinner was sent in from the restaurant. Orlov asked her not to broach the question of moving until after they had come back from abroad, and apropos of their foreign tour, declared that they could not go till his hair had grown long, as one could not go trailing from hotel to hotel and serving the idea without long hair.

To crown it all, in Orlov's absence, Kukushkin began calling at the flat in the evening. There was nothing exceptional in his behaviour, but I could never forget the conversation in which he had offered to cut Orlov out. He was regaled with tea and red wine, and he used to titter and, anxious to say something pleasant, would declare that a free union was superior in every respect to legal marriage, and that all decent people ought really to come to Zinaida Fyodorovna and fall at her feet.

VIII

Christmas was spent drearily in vague anticipations of calamity. On New Year's Eve Orlov unexpectedly announced at breakfast that he was being sent to assist a senator who was on a revising commission in a certain province.

"I don't want to go, but I can't find an excuse to get off," he said with vexation. "I must go; there's nothing for it."

Such news instantly made Zinaida Fyodorovna's eyes look red. "Is it for long?" she asked.

"Five days or so."

"I am glad, really, you are going," she said after a moment's thought. "It will be a change for you. You will fall in love with some one on the way, and tell me about it afterwards."

At every opportunity she tried to make Orlov feel that she did not restrict his liberty in any way, and that he could do exactly as he liked, and this artless, transparent strategy deceived no one, and only unnecessarily reminded Orlov that he was not free.

"I am going this evening," he said, and began reading the paper.

Zinaida Fyodorovna wanted to see him off at the station, but he dissuaded her, saying that he was not going to America, and not going to be away five years, but only five days -- possibly less.

The parting took place between seven and eight. He put one arm round her, and kissed her on the lips and on the forehead.

"Be a good girl, and don't be depressed while I am away," he said in a warm, affectionate tone which touched even me. "God keep you!"

She looked greedily into his face, to stamp his dear features on her memory, then she put her arms gracefully round his neck and laid her head on his breast.

"Forgive me our misunderstandings," she said in French. "Husband and wife cannot help quarrelling if they love each other, and I love you madly. Don't forget me. . . . Wire to me often and fully."

Orlov kissed her once more, and, without saying a word, went out in confusion. When he heard the click of the lock as the door closed, he stood still in the middle of the staircase in hesitation and glanced upwards. It seemed to me that if a sound had reached him at that moment from above, he would have turned back. But all was quiet. He straightened his coat and went downstairs irresolutely.

The sledges had been waiting a long while at the door. Orlov got into one, I got into the other with two portmanteaus. It was a hard frost and there were fires smoking at the cross-roads. The cold wind nipped my face and hands, and took my breath away as we drove rapidly along; and, closing my eyes, I thought what a splendid woman she was. How she loved him! Even useless rubbish is collected in the courtyards nowadays and used for some purpose, even broken glass is considered a useful commodity, but something so precious, so rare, as the love of a refined, young, intelligent, and good woman is utterly thrown away and wasted. One of the early sociologists regarded every evil passion as a force which might by judicious management be turned to good, while among us even a fine, noble passion springs up and dies away in impotence, turned to no account, misunderstood or vulgarised. Why is it?

The sledges stopped unexpectedly. I opened my eyes and I saw that we had come to a standstill in Sergievsky Street, near a big house where Pekarsky lived. Orlov got out of the sledge and vanished into the entry. Five minutes later Pekarsky's footman came out, bareheaded, and, angry with the frost, shouted to me:

"Are you deaf? Pay the cabmen and go upstairs. You are wanted!"

At a complete loss, I went to the first storey. I had been to Pekarsky's flat before -- that is, I had stood in the hall and looked into the drawing-room, and, after the damp, gloomy street, it always struck me by the brilliance of its picture-frames, its bronzes and expensive furniture. To-day in the midst of this splendour I saw Gruzin, Kukushkin, and, after a minute, Orlov.

"Look here, Stepan," he said, coming up to me. "I shall be staying here till Friday or Saturday. If any letters or telegrams come, you must bring them here every day. At home, of course you will say that I have gone, and send my greetings. Now you can go."

When I reached home Zinaida Fyodorovna was lying on the sofa in the drawing-room, eating a pear. There was only one candle burning in the candelabra.

"Did you catch the train?" asked Zinaida Fyodorovna.

"Yes, madam. His honour sends his greetings."

I went into my room and I, too, lay down. I had nothing to do, and I did not want to read. I was not surprised and I was not indignant. I only racked my brains to think why this deception was necessary. It is only boys in their teens who deceive their mistresses like that. How was it that a man who had thought and read so much could not imagine anything more sensible? I must confess I had by no means a poor opinion of his intelligence. I believe if he had had to deceive his minister or any other influential person he would have put a great deal of skill and energy into doing so; but to deceive a woman, the first idea that occurred to him was evidently good enough. If it succeeded -- well and good; if it did not, there would be no harm done -- he could tell some other lie just as quickly and simply, with no mental effort.

At midnight when the people on the floor overhead were moving their chairs and shouting hurrah to welcome the New Year, Zinaida Fyodorovna rang for me from the room next to the study. Languid from lying down so long, she was sitting at the table, writing something on a scrap of paper.

"I must send a telegram," she said, with a smile. "Go to the station as quick as you can and ask them to send it after him."

Going out into the street, I read on the scrap of paper:

"May the New Year bring new happiness. Make haste and telegraph; I miss you dreadfully. It seems an eternity. I am only sorry I can't send a thousand kisses and my very heart by telegraph. Enjoy yourself, my darling.-- ZINA."

I sent the telegram, and next morning I gave her the receipt.

IX

The worst of it was that Orlov had thoughtlessly let Polya, too, into the secret of his deception, telling her to bring his shirts to Sergievsky Street. After that, she looked at Zinaida Fyodorovna with a malignant joy and hatred I could not understand, and was never tired of snorting with delight to herself in her own room and in the hall.

"She's outstayed her welcome; it's time she took herself off!" she would say with zest. "She ought to realise that herself. . . ."

She already divined by instinct that Zinaida Fyodorovna would not be with us much longer, and, not to let the chance slip, carried off everything she set her eyes on -- smelling-bottles, tortoise-shell hairpins, handkerchiefs, shoes! On the day after New Year's Day, Zinaida Fyodorovna summoned me to her room and told me in a low voice that she missed her black dress. And then she walked through all the rooms, with a pale, frightened, and indignant face, talking to herself:

"It's too much! It's beyond everything. Why, it's unheard-of insolence!"

At dinner she tried to help herself to soup, but could not -- her hands were trembling. Her lips were trembling, too. She looked helplessly at the soup and at the little pies, waiting for the trembling to pass off, and suddenly she could not resist looking at Polya.

"You can go, Polya," she said. "Stepan is enough by himself."

"I'll stay; I don't mind," answered Polya.

"There's no need for you to stay. You go away altogether," Zinaida Fyodorovna went on, getting up in great agitation. "You may look out for another place. You can go at once."

"I can't go away without the master's orders. He engaged me. It must be as he orders."

"You can take orders from me, too! I am mistress here!" said Zinaida Fyodorovna, and she flushed crimson.

"You may be the mistress, but only the master can dismiss me. It was he engaged me."

"You dare not stay here another minute!" cried Zinaida Fyodorovna, and she struck the plate with her knife. "You are a thief! Do you hear?"

Zinaida Fyodorovna flung her dinner-napkin on the table, and with a pitiful, suffering face, went quickly out of the room. Loudly sobbing and wailing something indistinct, Polya, too, went away. The soup and the grouse got cold. And for some reason all the restaurant dainties on the table struck me as poor, thievish, like Polya. Two pies on a plate had a particularly miserable and guilty air. "We shall be taken back to the restaurant to-day," they seemed to be saying, "and to-morrow we shall be put on the table again for some official or celebrated singer."

"She is a fine lady, indeed," I heard uttered in Polya's room. "I could have been a lady like that long ago, but I have some self-respect! We'll see which of us will be the first to go!"

Zinaida Fyodorovna rang the bell. She was sitting in her room, in the corner, looking as though she had been put in the corner as a punishment.

"No telegram has come?" she asked.

"No, madam."

"Ask the porter; perhaps there is a telegram. And don't leave the house," she called after me. "I am afraid to be left alone."

After that I had to run down almost every hour to ask the porter whether a telegram had come. I must own it was a dreadful time! To avoid seeing Polya, Zinaida Fyodorovna dined and had tea in her own room; it was here that she slept, too, on a short sofa like a half-moon, and she made her own bed. For the first days I took the telegrams; but, getting no answer, she lost her faith in me and began telegraphing herself. Looking at her, I, too, began impatiently hoping for a telegram. I hoped he would contrive some deception, would make arrangements, for instance, that a telegram should be sent to her from some station. If he were too much engrossed with cards or had been attracted by some other woman, I thought that both Gruzin and Kukushkin would remind him of us. But our expectations were vain. Five times a day I would go in to Zinaida Fyodorovna, intending to tell her the truth, But her eyes looked piteous as a fawn's, her shoulders seemed to droop, her lips were moving, and I went away again without saying a word. Pity and sympathy seemed to rob me of all manliness. Polya, as cheerful and well satisfied with herself as though nothing had happened, was tidying the master's study and the bedroom, rummaging in the cupboards, and making the crockery jingle, and when she passed Zinaida Fyodorovna's door, she hummed something and coughed. She was pleased that her mistress was hiding from her. In the evening she would go out somewhere, and rang at two or three o'clock in the morning, and I had to open the door to her and listen to remarks about my cough. Immediately afterwards I would hear another ring; I would run to the room next to the study, and Zinaida Fyodorovna, putting her head out of the door, would ask, "Who was it rung?" while she looked at my hands to see whether I had a telegram.

When at last on Saturday the bell rang below and she heard the familiar voice on the stairs, she was so delighted that she broke into sobs. She rushed to meet him, embraced him, kissed him on the breast and sleeves, said something one could not understand. The hall porter brought up the portmanteaus; Polya's cheerful voice was heard. It was as though some one had come home for the holidays.

"Why didn't you wire?" asked Zinaida Fyodorovna, breathless with joy. "Why was it? I have been in misery; I don't know how I've lived through it. . . . Oh, my God!"

"It was very simple! I returned with the senator to Moscow the very first day, and didn't get your telegrams," said Orlov. "After dinner, my love, I'll give you a full account of my doings, but now I must sleep and sleep. . . . I am worn out with the journey."

It was evident that he had not slept all night; he had probably been playing cards and drinking freely. Zinaida Fyodorovna put him to bed, and we all walked about on tiptoe all that day. The dinner went off quite satisfactorily, but when they went into the study and had coffee the explanation began. Zinaida Fyodorovna began talking of something rapidly in a low voice; she spoke in French, and her words flowed like a stream. Then I heard a loud sigh from Orlov, and his voice.

"My God!" he said in French. "Have you really nothing fresher to tell me than this everlasting tale of your servant's misdeeds?"

"But, my dear, she robbed me and said insulting things to me."

"But why is it she doesn't rob me or say insulting things to me? Why is it I never notice the maids nor the porters nor the footmen? My dear, you are simply capricious and refuse to know your own mind. . . . I really begin to suspect that you must be in a certain condition. When I offered to let her go, you insisted on her remaining, and now you want me to turn her away. I can be obstinate, too, in such cases. You want her to go, but I want her to remain. That's the only way to cure you of your nerves."

"Oh, very well, very well," said Zinaida Fyodorovna in alarm. "Let us say no more about that. . . . Let us put it off till to-morrow. . . . Now tell me about Moscow. . . . What is going on in Moscow?"

X

After lunch next day -- it was the seventh of January, St. John the Baptist's Day -- Orlov put on his black dress coat and his decoration to go to visit his father and congratulate him on his name day. He had to go at two o'clock, and it was only half-past one when he had finished dressing. What was he to do for that half-hour? He walked about the drawing-room, declaiming some congratulatory verses which he had recited as a child to his father and mother.

Zinaida Fyodorovna, who was just going out to a dressmaker's or to the shops, was sitting, listening to him with a smile. I don't know how their conversation began, but when I took Orlov his gloves, he was standing before her with a capricious, beseeching face, saying:

"For God's sake, in the name of everything that's holy, don't talk of things that everybody knows! What an unfortunate gift our intellectual thoughtful ladies have for talking with enthusiasm and an air of profundity of things that every schoolboy is sick to death of! Ah, if only you would exclude from our conjugal programme all these serious questions! How grateful I should be to you!"

"We women may not dare, it seems, to have views of our own."

46

"I give you full liberty to be as liberal as you like, and quote from any authors you choose, but make me one concession: don't hold forth in my presence on either of two subjects: the corruption of the upper classes and the evils of the marriage system. Do understand me, at last. The upper class is always abused in contrast with the world of tradesmen, priests, workmen and peasants, Sidors and Nikitas of all sorts. I detest both classes, but if I had honestly to choose between the two, I should without hesitation, prefer the upper class, and there would be no falsity or affectation about it, since all my tastes are in that direction. Our world is trivial and empty, but at any rate we speak French decently, read something, and don't punch each other in the ribs even in our most violent quarrels, while the Sidors and the Nikitas and their worships in trade talk about 'being quite agreeable,' 'in a jiffy,' 'blast your eyes,' and display the utmost license of pothouse manners and the most degrading superstition."

"The peasant and the tradesman feed you."

"Yes, but what of it? That's not only to my discredit, but to theirs too. They feed me and take off their caps to me, so it seems they have not the intelligence and honesty to do otherwise. I don't blame or praise any one: I only mean that the upper class and the lower are as bad as one another. My feelings and my intelligence are opposed to both, but my tastes lie more in the direction of the former. Well, now for the evils of marriage," Orlov went on, glancing at his watch. "It's high time for you to understand that there are no evils in the system itself; what is the matter is that you don't know yourselves what you want from marriage. What is it you want? In legal and illegal cohabitation, in every sort of union and cohabitation, good or bad, the underlying reality is the same. You ladies live for that underlying reality alone: for you it's everything; your existence would have no meaning for you without it. You want nothing but that, and you get it; but since you've taken to reading novels you are ashamed of it: you rush from pillar to post, you recklessly change your men, and to justify this turmoil you have begun talking of the evils of marriage. So long as you can't and won't renounce what underlies it all, your chief foe, your devil -- so long as you serve that slavishly, what use is there in discussing the matter seriously? Everything you may say to me will be falsity and affectation. I shall not believe you."

I went to find out from the hall porter whether the sledge was at the door, and when I came back I found it had become a quarrel. As sailors say, a squall had blown up.

"I see you want to shock me by your cynicism today," said Zinaida Fyodorovna, walking about the drawing-room in great emotion. "It revolts me to listen to you. I am pure before God and man, and have nothing to repent of. I left my husband and came to you, and am proud of it. I swear, on my honour, I am proud of it!"

"Well, that's all right, then!"

"If you are a decent, honest man, you, too, ought to be proud of what I did. It raises you and me above thousands of people who would like to do as we have done, but do not venture through cowardice or petty prudence. But you are not a decent man. You are afraid of freedom, and you mock the promptings of genuine feeling, from fear that some ignoramus may suspect you of being sincere. You are afraid to show me to your friends; there's no greater infliction for you than to go about with me in the street. . . . Isn't that true? Why haven't you introduced me to your father or your cousin all this time? Why is it? No, I am sick of it at last," cried Zinaida Fyodorovna, stamping. "I demand what is mine by right. You must present me to your father."

"If you want to know him, go and present yourself. He receives visitors every morning from ten till half-past."

"How base you are!" said Zinaida Fyodorovna, wringing her hands in despair. "Even if you are not sincere, and are not saying what you think, I might hate you for your cruelty. Oh, how base you are!"

"We keep going round and round and never reach the real point. The real point is that you made a mistake, and you won't acknowledge it aloud. You imagined that I was a hero, and that I had some extraordinary ideas and ideals, and it has turned out that I am a most ordinary official, a cardplayer, and have no partiality for ideas of any sort. I am a worthy representative of the rotten world from which you have run away because you were revolted with its triviality and emptiness. Recognise it and be just: don't be indignant with me, but with yourself, as it is your mistake, and not mine."

"Yes, I admit I was mistaken."

"Well, that's all right, then. We've reached that point at last, thank God. Now hear something more, if you please: I can't rise to your level -- I am too depraved; you can't descend to my level, either, for you are too exalted. So there is only one thing left to do. . . ."

"What?" Zinaida Fyodorovna asked quickly, holding her breath and turning suddenly as white as a sheet of paper.

"To call logic to our aid. . . ."

"Georgy, why are you torturing me?" Zinaida Fyodorovna said suddenly in Russian in a breaking voice. "What is it for? Think of my misery. . . ."

Orlov, afraid of tears, went quickly into his study, and I don't know why -- whether it was that he wished to cause her extra pain, or whether he remembered it was usually done in such cases -- he locked the door after him. She cried out and ran after him with a rustle of her skirt.

"What does this mean?" she cried, knocking at his door. "What . . . what does this mean?" she repeated in a shrill voice breaking with indignation. "Ah, so this is what you do! Then let me tell you I hate you, I despise you! Everything is over between us now."

I heard hysterical weeping mingled with laughter. Something small in the drawing-room fell off the table and was broken. Orlov went out into the hall by another door, and, looking round him nervously, he hurriedly put on his great-coat and went out.

Half an hour passed, an hour, and she was still weeping. I remembered that she had no father or mother, no relations, and here she was living between a man who hated her and Polya, who robbed her -- and how desolate her life seemed to me! I do not know why, but I went into the drawing-room to her. Weak and helpless, looking with her lovely hair like an embodiment of tenderness and grace, she was in anguish, as though she were ill; she was lying on a couch, hiding her face, and quivering all over.

"Madam, shouldn't I fetch a doctor?" I asked gently.

"No, there's no need . . . it's nothing," she said, and she looked at me with her tear-stained eyes. "I have a little headache. . . . Thank you."

I went out, and in the evening she was writing letter after letter, and sent me out first to Pekarsky, then to Gruzin, then to Kukushkin, and finally anywhere I chose, if only I could find Orlov and give him the letter. Every time I came back with the letter she scolded me, entreated me, thrust money into my hand -- as though she were in a fever. And all the night she did not sleep, but sat in the drawing-room, talking to herself.

Orlov returned to dinner next day, and they were reconciled.

The first Thursday afterwards Orlov complained to his friends of the intolerable life he led; he smoked a great deal, and said with irritation:

"It is no life at all; it's the rack. Tears, wailing, intellectual conversations, begging for forgiveness, again tears and wailing; and the long and the short of it is that I have no flat of my own now. I am wretched, and I make her wretched. Surely I haven't to live another month or two like this? How can I? But yet I may have to."

"Why don't you speak, then?" said Pekarsky.

"I've tried, but I can't. One can boldly tell the truth, whatever it may be, to an independent, rational man; but in this case one has to do with a creature who has no will, no strength of character, and no logic. I cannot endure tears; they disarm me. When she cries, I am ready to swear eternal love and cry myself."

Pekarsky did not understand; he scratched his broad forehead in perplexity and said:

"You really had better take another flat for her. It's so simple!"

"She wants me, not the flat. But what's the good of talking?" sighed Orlov. "I only hear endless conversations, but no way out of my position. It certainly is a case of 'being guilty without guilt.' I don't claim to be a mushroom, but it seems I've got to go into the basket. The last thing I've ever set out to be is a hero. I never could endure Turgenev's novels; and now, all of a sudden, as though to spite me, I've heroism forced upon me. I assure her on my honour that I'm not a hero at all, I adduce irrefutable proofs of the same, but she doesn't believe me. Why doesn't she believe me? I suppose I really must have something of the appearance of a hero."

"You go off on a tour of inspection in the provinces," said Kukushkin, laughing.

"Yes, that's the only thing left for me."

A week after this conversation Orlov announced that he was again ordered to attend the senator, and the same evening he went off with his portmanteaus to Pekarsky.

XI

An old man of sixty, in a long fur coat reaching to the ground, and a beaver cap, was standing at the door.

"Is Georgy Ivanitch at home?" he asked.

At first I thought it was one of the moneylenders, Gruzin's creditors, who sometimes used to come to Orlov for small payments on account; but when he came into the hall and flung open his coat, I saw the thick brows and the characteristically compressed lips which I knew so well from the photographs, and two rows of stars on the uniform. I recognised him: it was Orlov's father, the distinguished statesman.

I answered that Georgy Ivanitch was not at home. The old man pursed up his lips tightly and looked into space, reflecting, showing me his dried-up, toothless profile.

51

"I'll leave a note," he said; "show me in."

He left his goloshes in the hall, and, without taking off his long, heavy fur coat, went into the study. There he sat down before the table, and, before taking up the pen, for three minutes he pondered, shading his eyes with his hand as though from the sun -- exactly as his son did when he was out of humour. His face was sad, thoughtful, with that look of resignation which I have only seen on the faces of the old and religious. I stood behind him, gazed at his bald head and at the hollow at the nape of his neck, and it was clear as daylight to me that this weak old man was now in my power. There was not a soul in the flat except my enemy and me. I had only to use a little physical violence, then snatch his watch to disguise the object of the crime, and to get off by the back way, and I should have gained infinitely more than I could have imagined possible when I took up the part of a footman. I thought that I could hardly get a better opportunity. But instead of acting, I looked quite unconcernedly, first at his bald patch and then at his fur, and calmly meditated on this man's relation to his only son, and on the fact that people spoiled by power and wealth probably don't want to die. . . .

"Have you been long in my son's service?" he asked, writing a large hand on the paper.

"Three months, your High Excellency."

He finished the letter and stood up. I still had time. I urged myself on and clenched my fists, trying to wring out of my soul some trace of my former hatred; I recalled what a passionate, implacable, obstinate hate I had felt for him only a little while before. . . . But it is difficult to strike a match against a crumbling stone. The sad old face and the cold glitter of his stars roused in me nothing but petty, cheap, unnecessary thoughts of the transitoriness of everything earthly, of the nearness of death. . . .

"Good-day, brother," said the old man. He put on his cap and went out.

There could be no doubt about it: I had undergone a change; I had become different. To convince myself, I began to recall the past, but at once I felt uneasy, as though I had accidentally peeped into a dark, damp corner. I remembered my comrades and friends, and my first thought was how I should blush in confusion if ever I met any of them. What was I now? What had I to think of and to do? Where was I to go? What was I living for?

I could make nothing of it. I only knew one thing -- that I must make haste to pack my things and be off. Before the old man's visit my position as a flunkey had a meaning; now it was absurd. Tears dropped into my open portmanteau; I felt insufferably sad; but how I longed to live! I was ready to embrace and include in my short life every possibility open to man. I wanted to speak, to read, and to hammer in some big factory, and to stand on watch, and to plough. I yearned for the Nevsky Prospect, for the sea and the fields -- for every place to which my imagination travelled. When Zinaida Fyodorovna came in, I rushed to open the door for her, and with peculiar tenderness took off her fur coat. The last time!

We had two other visitors that day besides the old man. In the evening when it was quite dark, Gruzin came to fetch some papers for Orlov. He opened the table-drawer, took the necessary papers, and, rolling them up, told me to put them in the hall beside his cap while he went in to see Zinaida Fyodorovna. She was lying on the sofa in the drawing-room, with her arms behind her head. Five or six days had already passed since Orlov went on his tour of inspection, and no one knew when he would be back, but this time she did not send telegrams and did not expect them. She did not seem to notice the presence of Polya, who was still living with us. "So be it, then," was what I read on her passionless and very pale face. Like Orlov, she wanted to be unhappy out of obstinacy. To spite herself and everything in the world, she lay for days together on the sofa, desiring and expecting nothing but evil for herself. Probably she was picturing to herself Orlov's return and the inevitable quarrels with him; then his growing indifference to her, his infidelities; then how they would separate; and perhaps these agonising thoughts gave her satisfaction. But what would she have said if she found out the actual truth?

"I love you, Godmother," said Gruzin, greeting her and kissing her hand. "You are so kind! And so dear George has gone away," he lied. "He has gone away, the rascal!"

He sat down with a sigh and tenderly stroked her hand.

"Let me spend an hour with you, my dear," he said. "I don't want to go home, and it's too early to go to the Birshovs'. The Birshovs are keeping their Katya's birthday to-day. She is a nice child!"

I brought him a glass of tea and a decanter of brandy. He slowly and with obvious reluctance drank the tea, and returning the glass to me, asked timidly:

"Can you give me . . . something to eat, my friend? I have had no dinner."

We had nothing in the flat. I went to the restaurant and brought him the ordinary rouble dinner.

"To your health, my dear," he said to Zinaida Fyodorovna, and he tossed off a glass of vodka. "My little girl, your godchild, sends you her love. Poor child! she's rickety. Ah, children, children!" he sighed. "Whatever you may say, Godmother, it is nice to be a father. Dear George can't understand that feeling."

He drank some more. Pale and lean, with his dinner-napkin over his chest like a little pinafore, he ate greedily, and raising his eyebrows, kept looking guiltily, like a little boy, first at Zinaida Fyodorovna and then at me. It seemed as though he would have begun crying if I had not given him the grouse or the jelly. When he had satisfied his hunger he grew more lively, and began laughingly telling some story about the Birshov household, but perceiving that it was tiresome and that Zinaida Fyodorovna was not laughing, he ceased. And there was a sudden feeling of dreariness. After he had finished his dinner they sat in the drawing-room by the light of a single lamp, and did not speak; it was painful to him to lie to her, and she wanted to ask him something, but could not make up her mind to. So passed half an hour. Gruzin glanced at his watch.

"I suppose it's time for me to go."

"No, stay a little. . . . We must have a talk."

Again they were silent. He sat down to the piano, struck one chord, then began playing, and sang softly, "What does the coming day bring me?" but as usual he got up suddenly and tossed his head.

"Play something," Zinaida Fyodorovna asked him.

"What shall I play?" he asked, shrugging his shoulders. "I have forgotten everything. I've given it up long ago."

Looking at the ceiling as though trying to remember, he played two pieces of Tchaikovsky with exquisite expression, with such warmth, such insight! His face was just as usual -- neither stupid nor intelligent -- and it seemed to me a perfect marvel that a man whom I was accustomed to see in the midst of the most degrading, impure surroundings, was capable of such purity, of rising to a feeling so lofty, so far beyond my reach. Zinaida Fyodorovna's face glowed, and she walked about the drawing-room in emotion.

"Wait a bit, Godmother; if I can remember it, I will play you something," he said; "I heard it played on the violoncello."

Beginning timidly and picking out the notes, and then gathering confidence, he played Saint-Saëns's "Swan Song." He played it through, and then played it a second time.

"It's nice, isn't it?" he said.

Moved by the music, Zinaida Fyodorovna stood beside him and asked:

"Tell me honestly, as a friend, what do you think about me?"

"What am I to say?" he said, raising his eyebrows. "I love you and think nothing but good of you. But if you wish that I should speak generally about the question that interests you," he went on, rubbing his sleeve near the elbow and frowning, "then, my dear, you know. .

. . To follow freely the promptings of the heart does not always give good people happiness. To feel free and at the same time to be happy, it seems to me, one must not conceal from oneself that life is coarse, cruel, and merciless in its conservatism, and one must retaliate with what it deserves -- that is, be as coarse and as merciless in one's striving for freedom. That's what I think."

"That's beyond me," said Zinaida Fyodorovna, with a mournful smile. "I am exhausted already. I am so exhausted that I wouldn't stir a finger for my own salvation."

"Go into a nunnery."

He said this in jest, but after he had said it, tears glistened in Zinaida Fyodorovna's eyes and then in his.

"Well," he said, "we've been sitting and sitting, and now we must go. Good-bye, dear Godmother. God give you health."

He kissed both her hands, and stroking them tenderly, said that he should certainly come to see her again in a day or two. In the hall, as he was putting on his overcoat, that was so like a child's pelisse, he fumbled long in his pockets to find a tip for me, but found nothing there.

"Good-bye, my dear fellow," he said sadly, and went away.

I shall never forget the feeling that this man left behind him.

Zinaida Fyodorovna still walked about the room in her excitement. That she was walking about and not still lying down was so much to the good. I wanted to take advantage of this mood to speak to her openly and then to go away, but I had hardly seen Gruzin out when I heard a ring. It was Kukushkin.

"Is Georgy Ivanitch at home?" he said. "Has he come back? You say no? What a pity! In that case, I'll go in and kiss your mistress's hand, and so away. Zinaida Fyodorovna, may I come in?" he cried. "I want to kiss your hand. Excuse my being so late."

He was not long in the drawing-room, not more than ten minutes, but I felt as though he were staying a long while and would never go away. I bit my lips from indignation and annoyance, and already hated Zinaida Fyodorovna. "Why does she not turn him out?" I thought indignantly, though it was evident that she was bored by his company.

When I held his fur coat for him he asked me, as a mark of special good-will, how I managed to get on without a wife.

"But I don't suppose you waste your time," he said, laughingly. "I've no doubt Polya and you are as thick as thieves. . . . You rascal!"

In spite of my experience of life, I knew very little of mankind at that time, and it is very likely that I often exaggerated what was of little consequence and failed to observe what was important. It seemed to me it was not without motive that Kukushkin tittered and flattered me. Could it be that he was hoping that I, like a flunkey, would gossip in other kitchens and servants' quarters of his coming to see us in the evenings when Orlov was away, and staying with Zinaida Fyodorovna till late at night? And when my tittle-tattle came to the ears of his acquaintance, he would drop his eyes in confusion and shake his little finger. And would not he, I thought, looking at his little honeyed face, this very evening at cards pretend and perhaps declare that he had already won Zinaida Fyodorovna from Orlov?

That hatred which failed me at midday when the old father had come, took possession of me now. Kukushkin went away at last, and as I listened to the shuffle of his leather goloshes, I felt greatly tempted to fling after him, as a parting shot, some coarse word of abuse, but I restrained myself. And when the steps had died away on the stairs, I went back to the hall, and, hardly conscious of what I was doing, took up the roll of papers that Gruzin had left behind, and ran headlong downstairs. Without cap or overcoat, I ran down into the street. It was not cold, but big flakes of snow were falling and it was windy.

"Your Excellency!" I cried, catching up Kukushkin. "Your Excellency!

57

He stopped under a lamp-post and looked round with surprise. "Your Excellency!" I said breathless, "your Excellency!"

And not able to think of anything to say, I hit him two or three times on the face with the roll of paper. Completely at a loss, and hardly wondering-- I had so completely taken him by surprise -- he leaned his back against the lamp-post and put up his hands to protect his face. At that moment an army doctor passed, and saw how I was beating the man, but he merely looked at us in astonishment and went on. I felt ashamed and I ran back to the house.

XII

With my head wet from the snow, and gasping for breath, I ran to my room, and immediately flung off my swallow-tails, put on a reefer jacket and an overcoat, and carried my portmanteau out into the passage; I must get away! But before going I hurriedly sat down and began writing to Orlov:

"I leave you my false passport," I began. "I beg you to keep it as a memento, you false man, you Petersburg official!

"To steal into another man's house under a false name, to watch under the mask of a flunkey this person's intimate life, to hear everything, to see everything in order later on, unasked, to accuse a man of lying -- all this, you will say, is on a level with theft. Yes, but I care nothing for fine feelings now. I have endured dozens of your dinners and suppers when you said and did what you liked, and I had to hear, to look on, and be silent. I don't want to make you a present of my silence. Besides, if there is not a living soul at hand who dares to tell you the truth without flattery, let your flunkey Stepan wash your magnificent countenance for you."

I did not like this beginning, but I did not care to alter it. Besides, what did it matter?

The big windows with their dark curtains, the bed, the crumpled dress coat on the floor, and my wet footprints, looked gloomy and forbidding. And there was a peculiar stillness.

Possibly because I had run out into the street without my cap and goloshes I was in a high fever. My face burned, my legs ached. . . . My heavy head drooped over the table, and there was that kind of division in my thought when every idea in the brain seemed dogged by its shadow.

"I am ill, weak, morally cast down," I went on; "I cannot write to you as I should like to. From the first moment I desired to insult and humiliate you, but now I do not feel that I have the right to do so. You and I have both fallen, and neither of us will ever rise up again; and even if my letter were eloquent, terrible, and passionate, it would still seem like beating on the lid of a coffin: however one knocks upon it, one will not wake up the dead! No efforts could warm your accursed cold blood, and you know that better than I do. Why write? But my mind and heart are burning, and I go on writing; for some reason I am moved as though this letter still might save you and me. I am so feverish that my thoughts are disconnected, and my pen scratches the paper without meaning; but the question I want to put to you stands before me as clear as though in letters of flame.

"Why I am prematurely weak and fallen is not hard to explain. Like Samson of old, I have taken the gates of Gaza on my shoulders to carry them to the top of the mountain, and only when I was exhausted, when youth and health were quenched in me forever, I noticed that that burden was not for my shoulders, and that I had deceived myself. I have been, moreover, in cruel and continual pain. I have endured cold, hunger, illness, and loss of liberty. Of personal happiness I know and have known nothing. I have no home; my memories are bitter, and my conscience is often in dread of them. But why have you fallen -- you? What fatal, diabolical causes hindered your life from blossoming into full flower? Why, almost before beginning life, were you in such haste to cast off the image and likeness of God, and to become a cowardly beast who backs and scares others because he is afraid himself? You are afraid of life -- as afraid of it as an Oriental who sits all day on a cushion smoking his hookah. Yes, you read a great deal, and a European coat fits you well, but yet with what tender, purely Oriental, pasha-like care you protect yourself from hunger, cold, physical effort, from pain and uneasiness! How early your soul has taken to its dressing-gown! What a cowardly part you have played towards real life and nature, with which every healthy and normal man struggles! How soft, how snug, how warm, how comfortable -- and how bored you are! Yes, it is deathly boredom, unrelieved by one ray of light, as in solitary confinement; but you try to hide from that enemy, too, you play cards eight hours out of twenty-four.

"And your irony? Oh, but how well I understand it! Free, bold, living thought is searching and dominating; for an indolent, sluggish mind it is intolerable. That it may not disturb your peace, like thousands of your contemporaries, you made haste in youth to put it under bar and bolt. Your ironical attitude to life, or whatever you like to call it, is your armour; and your thought, fettered and frightened, dare not leap over the fence you have put round it; and when you jeer at ideas which you pretend to know all about, you are like the deserter fleeing from the field of battle, and, to stifle his shame, sneering at war and at valour. Cynicism stifles pain. In some novel of Dostoevsky's an old man tramples underfoot the portrait of his dearly loved daughter because he had been unjust to her, and you vent your foul and vulgar jeers upon the ideas of goodness and truth because you have not the strength to follow them. You are frightened of every honest and truthful hint at your degradation, and you purposely surround yourself with people who do nothing but flatter your weaknesses. And you may well, you may well dread the sight of tears!

"By the way, your attitude to women. Shamelessness has been handed down to us in our flesh and blood, and we are trained to shamelessness; but that is what we are men for -- to subdue the beast in us. When you reached manhood and all ideas became known to you, you could not have failed to see the truth; you knew it, but you did not follow it; you were afraid of it, and to deceive your conscience you began loudly assuring yourself that it was not you but woman that was to blame, that she was as degraded as your attitude to her. Your cold, scabrous anecdotes, your coarse laughter, all your innumerable theories concerning the underlying reality of marriage and the definite demands made upon it, concerning the ten sous the French workman pays his woman; your everlasting attacks on female logic, lying, weakness and so on -- doesn't it all look like a desire at all costs to force woman down into the mud that she may be on the same level as your attitude to her? You are a weak, unhappy, unpleasant person!"

Zinaida Fyodorovna began playing the piano in the drawing-room, trying to recall the song of Saint Saëns that Gruzin had played. I went and lay on my bed, but remembering that it was time for me to go, I got up with an effort and with a heavy, burning head went to the table again.

"But this is the question," I went on. "Why are we worn out? Why are we, at first so passionate so bold, so noble, and so full of faith, complete bankrupts at thirty or thirty-five? Why does one waste in consumption, another put a bullet through his brains, a third seeks forgetfulness in vodka and cards, while the fourth tries to stifle his fear and misery by cynically trampling underfoot the pure image of his fair youth? Why is it that, having once fallen, we do not try to rise up again, and, losing one thing, do not seek something else? Why is it?

"The thief hanging on the Cross could bring back the joy of life and the courage of confident hope, though perhaps he had not more than an hour to live. You have long years before you, and I shall probably not die so soon as one might suppose. What if by a miracle the present turned out to be a dream, a horrible nightmare, and we should wake up renewed, pure, strong, proud of our righteousness? Sweet visions fire me, and I am almost breathless with emotion. I have a terrible longing to live. I long for our life to be holy, lofty, and majestic as the heavens above. Let us live! The sun doesn't rise twice a day, and life is not given us again -- clutch at what is left of your life and save it. . . ."

I did not write another word. I had a multitude of thoughts in my mind, but I could not connect them and get them on to paper. Without finishing the letter, I signed it with my name and rank, and went into the study. It was dark. I felt for the table and put the letter on it. I must have stumbled against the furniture in the dark and made a noise.

"Who is there?" I heard an alarmed voice in the drawing-room.

And the clock on the table softly struck one at the moment.

XIII

For at least half a minute I fumbled at the door in the dark, feeling for the handle; then I slowly opened it and walked into the drawing-room. Zinaida Fyodorovna was lying on the couch, and raising herself on her elbow, she looked towards me. Unable to bring myself to speak, I walked slowly by, and she followed me with her eyes. I stood for a little time in the dining-room and then walked by her again, and she looked at me intently and with perplexity, even with alarm. At last I stood still and said with an effort:

"He is not coming back."

She quickly got on to her feet, and looked at me without understanding.

"He is not coming back," I repeated, and my heart beat violently. "He will not come back, for he has not left Petersburg. He is staying at Pekarsky's."

She understood and believed me -- I saw that from her sudden pallor, and from the way she laid her arms upon her bosom in terror and entreaty. In one instant all that had happened of late flashed through her mind; she reflected, and with pitiless clarity she saw the whole truth. But at the same time she remembered that I was a flunkey, a being of a lower order. . . . A casual stranger, with hair ruffled, with face flushed with fever, perhaps drunk, in a common overcoat, was coarsely intruding into her intimate life, and that offended her. She said to me sternly:

"It's not your business: go away."

"Oh, believe me!" I cried impetuously, holding out my hands to her.

62

"I am not a footman; I am as free as you."

I mentioned my name, and, speaking very rapidly that she might not interrupt me or go away, explained to her who I was and why I was living there. This new discovery struck her more than the first. Till then she had hoped that her footman had lied or made a mistake or been silly, but now after my confession she had no doubts left. From the expression of her unhappy eyes and face, which suddenly lost its softness and beauty and looked old, I saw that she was insufferably miserable, and that the conversation would lead to no good; but I went on impetuously:

"The senator and the tour of inspection were invented to deceive you. In January, just as now, he did not go away, but stayed at Pekarsky's, and I saw him every day and took part in the deception. He was weary of you, he hated your presence here, he mocked at you. . . . If you could have heard how he and his friends here jeered at you and your love, you would not have remained here one minute! Go away from here! Go away."

"Well," she said in a shaking voice, and moved her hand over her hair. "Well, so be it."

Her eyes were full of tears, her lips were quivering, and her whole face was strikingly pale and distorted with anger. Orlov's coarse, petty lying revolted her and seemed to her contemptible, ridiculous: she smiled and I did not like that smile.

"Well," she repeated, passing her hand over her hair again, "so be it. He imagines that I shall die of humiliation, and instead of that I am . . . amused by it. There's no need for him to hide." She walked away from the piano and said, shrugging her shoulders: "There's no need. . . . It would have been simpler to have it out with me instead of keeping in hiding in other people's flats. I have eyes; I saw it myself long ago. . . . I was only waiting for him to come back to have things out once for all."

Then she sat down on a low chair by the table, and, leaning her head on the arm of the sofa, wept bitterly. In the drawing-room there was only one candle burning in the candelabra, and the chair where she was sitting was in darkness; but I saw how her head and shoulders were quivering, and how her hair, escaping from her combs, covered her neck, her face, her arms. . . . Her quiet, steady weeping, which was not hysterical but a woman's ordinary weeping, expressed a sense of insult, of wounded pride, of injury, and of something helpless, hopeless, which one could not set right and to which one could not get used. Her tears stirred an echo in my troubled and suffering heart; I forgot my illness and everything else in the world; I walked about the drawing-room and muttered distractedly:

"Is this life? . . . Oh, one can't go on living like this, one can't. . . . Oh, it's madness, wickedness, not life."

"What humiliation!" she said through her tears. "To live together, to smile at me at the very time when I was burdensome to him, ridiculous in his eyes! Oh, how humiliating!"

She lifted up her head, and looking at me with tear-stained eyes through her hair, wet with her tears, and pushing it back as it prevented her seeing me, she asked:

"They laughed at me?"

"To these men you were laughable -- you and your love and Turgenev; they said your head was full of him. And if we both die at once in despair, that will amuse them, too; they will make a funny anecdote of it and tell it at your requiem service. But why talk of them?" I said impatiently. "We must get away from here -- I cannot stay here one minute longer.

She began crying again, while I walked to the piano and sat down.

"What are we waiting for?" I asked dejectedly. "It's two o'clock."

"I am not waiting for anything," she said. "I am utterly lost."

"Why do you talk like that? We had better consider together what we are to do. Neither you nor I can stay here. Where do you intend to go?"

Suddenly there was a ring at the bell. My heart stood still. Could it be Orlov, to whom perhaps Kukushkin had complained of me? How should we meet? I went to open the door. It was Polya. She came in shaking the snow off her pelisse, and went into her room without saying a word to me. When I went back to the drawing-room, Zinaida Fyodorovna, pale as death, was standing in the middle of the room, looking towards me with big eyes.

"Who was it?" she asked softly.

"Polya," I answered.

She passed her hand over her hair and closed her eyes wearily.

"I will go away at once," she said. "Will you be kind and take me to the Petersburg Side? What time is it now?"

"A quarter to three."

XIV

When, a little afterwards, we went out of the house, it was dark and deserted in the street. Wet snow was falling and a damp wind lashed in one's face. I remember it was the beginning of March; a thaw had set in, and for some days past the cabmen had been driving on wheels. Under the impression of the back stairs, of the cold, of the midnight darkness, and the porter in his sheepskin who had questioned us before letting us out of the gate, Zinaida Fyodorovna was utterly cast down and dispirited. When we got into the cab and the hood was put up, trembling all over, she began hurriedly saying how grateful she was to me.

"I do not doubt your good-will, but I am ashamed that you should be troubled," she muttered. "Oh, I understand, I understand. . . . When Gruzin was here to-day, I felt that he was lying and concealing something. Well, so be it. But I am ashamed, anyway, that you should be troubled."

She still had her doubts. To dispel them finally, I asked the cabman to drive through Sergievsky Street; stopping him at Pekarsky's door, I got out of the cab and rang. When the porter came to the door, I asked aloud, that Zinaida Fyodorovna might hear, whether Georgy Ivanitch was at home.

"Yes," was the answer, "he came in half an hour ago. He must be in bed by now. What do you want?"

Zinaida Fyodorovna could not refrain from putting her head out.

"Has Georgy Ivanitch been staying here long?" she asked.

"Going on for three weeks."

"And he's not been away?"

"No," answered the porter, looking at me with surprise.

"Tell him, early to-morrow," I said, "that his sister has arrived from Warsaw. Good-bye."

Then we drove on. The cab had no apron, the snow fell on us in big flakes, and the wind, especially on the Neva, pierced us through and through. I began to feel as though we had been driving for a long time, that for ages we had been suffering, and that for ages I had been listening to Zinaida Fyodorovna's shuddering breath. In semi-delirium, as though half asleep, I looked back upon my strange, incoherent life, and for some reason recalled a melodrama, "The Parisian Beggars," which I had seen once or twice in my childhood. And when to shake off that semi-delirium I peeped out from the hood and saw the dawn, all the images of the past, all my misty thoughts, for some reason, blended in me into one distinct, overpowering thought: everything was irrevocably over for Zinaida Fyodorovna and for me. This was as certain a conviction as though the cold blue sky contained a prophecy, but a minute later I was already thinking of something else and believed differently.

"What am I now?" said Zinaida Fyodorovna, in a voice husky with the cold and the damp. "Where am I to go? What am I to do? Gruzin told me to go into a nunnery. Oh, I would! I would change my dress, my face, my name, my thoughts . . . everything -- everything, and would hide myself for ever. But they will not take me into a nunnery. I am with child."

"We will go abroad together to-morrow," I said.

"That's impossible. My husband won't give me a passport."

"I will take you without a passport."

The cabman stopped at a wooden house of two storeys, painted a dark colour. I rang. Taking from me her small light basket -- the only luggage we had brought with us -- Zinaida Fyodorovna gave a wry smile and said :

"These are my bijoux."

But she was so weak that she could not carry these bijoux.

It was a long while before the door was opened. After the third or fourth ring a light gleamed in the windows, and there was a sound of steps, coughing and whispering; at last the key grated in the lock, and a stout peasant woman with a frightened red face appeared at the door. Some distance behind her stood a thin little old woman with short grey hair, carrying a candle in her hand. Zinaida Fyodorovna ran into the passage and flung her arms round the old woman's neck.

"Nina, I've been deceived," she sobbed loudly. "I've been coarsely, foully deceived! Nina, Nina!"

I handed the basket to the peasant woman. The door was closed, but still I heard her sobs and the cry "Nina!"

I got into the cab and told the man to drive slowly to the Nevsky Prospect. I had to think of a night's lodging for myself.

Next day towards evening I went to see Zinaida Fyodorovna. She was terribly changed. There were no traces of tears on her pale, terribly sunken face, and her expression was different. I don't know whether it was that I saw her now in different surroundings, far from luxurious, and that our relations were by now different, or perhaps that intense grief had already set its mark upon her; she did not strike me as so elegant and well dressed as before. Her figure seemed smaller; there was an abruptness and excessive nervousness about her as though she were in a hurry, and there was not the same softness even in her smile. I was dressed in an expensive suit which I had bought during the day. She looked first of all at that suit and at the hat in my hand, then turned an impatient, searching glance upon my face as though studying it.

"Your transformation still seems to me a sort of miracle," she said. "Forgive me for looking at you with such curiosity. You are an extraordinary man, you know."

I told her again who I was, and why I was living at Orlov's, and I told her at greater length and in more detail than the day before. She listened with great attention, and said without letting me finish:

"Everything there is over for me. You know, I could not refrain from writing a letter. Here is the answer."

On the sheet which she gave there was written in Orlov's hand:

"I am not going to justify myself. But you must own that it was your mistake, not mine. I wish you happiness, and beg you to make haste and forget.

Yours sincerely,

"G. O.

"P. S. -- I am sending on your things."

The trunks and baskets despatched by Orlov were standing in the passage, and my poor little portmanteau was there beside them.

"So . . ." Zinaida Fyodorovna began, but she did not finish.

68

We were silent. She took the note and held it for a couple of minutes before her eyes, and during that time her face wore the same haughty, contemptuous, proud, and harsh expression as the day before at the beginning of our explanation; tears came into her eyes -- not timid, bitter tears, but proud, angry tears.

"Listen," she said, getting up abruptly and moving away to the window that I might not see her face. "I have made up my mind to go abroad with you tomorrow."

"I am very glad. I am ready to go to-day."

"Accept me as a recruit. Have you read Balzac?" she asked suddenly, turning round. "Have you? At the end of his novel 'Père Goriot' the hero looks down upon Paris from the top of a hill and threatens the town: 'Now we shall settle our account,' and after this he begins a new life. So when I look out of the train window at Petersburg for the last time, I shall say, 'Now we shall settle our account!' "

Saying this, she smiled at her jest, and for some reason shuddered all over.

XV

At Venice I had an attack of pleurisy. Probably I had caught cold in the evening when we were rowing from the station to the Hotel Bauer. I had to take to my bed and stay there for a fortnight. Every morning while I was ill Zinaida Fyodorovna came from her room to drink coffee with me, and afterwards read aloud to me French and Russian books, of which we had bought a number at Vienna. These books were either long, long familiar to me or else had no interest for me, but I had the sound of a sweet, kind voice beside me, so that the meaning of all of them was summed up for me in the one thing -- I was not alone. She would go out for a walk, come back in her light grey dress, her light straw hat, gay, warmed by the spring sun; and sitting by my bed, bending low down over me, would tell me something about Venice or read me those books -- and I was happy.

At night I was cold, ill, and dreary, but by day I revelled in life -- I can find no better expression for it. The brilliant warm sunshine beating in at the open windows and at the door upon the balcony, the shouts below, the splash of oars, the tinkle of bells, the prolonged boom of the cannon at midday, and the feeling of perfect, perfect freedom, did wonders with me; I felt as though I were growing strong, broad wings which were bearing me God knows whither. And what charm, what joy at times at the thought that another life was so close to mine! that I was the servant, the guardian, the friend, the indispensable fellow-traveller of a creature, young, beautiful, wealthy, but weak, lonely, and insulted! It is pleasant even to be ill when you know that there are people who are looking forward to your convalescence as to a holiday. One day I heard her whispering behind the door with my doctor, and then she came in to me with tear-stained eyes. It was a bad sign, but I was touched, and there was a wonderful lightness in my heart.

But at last they allowed me to go out on the balcony. The sunshine and the breeze from the sea caressed and fondled my sick body. I looked down at the familiar gondolas, which glide with feminine grace smoothly and majestically as though they were alive, and felt all the luxury of this original, fascinating civilisation. There was a smell of the sea. Some one was playing a stringed instrument and two voices were singing. How delightful it was! How unlike it was to that Petersburg night when the wet snow was falling and beating so rudely on our faces. If one looks straight across the canal, one sees the sea, and on the wide expanse towards the horizon the sun glittered on the water so dazzlingly that it hurt one's eyes to look at it. My soul yearned towards that lovely sea, which was so akin to me and to which I had given up my youth. I longed to live -- to live -- and nothing more.

A fortnight later I began walking freely. I loved to sit in the sun, and to listen to the gondoliers without understanding them, and for hours together to gaze at the little house where, they said, Desdemona lived -- a naïve, mournful little house with a demure expression, as light as lace, so light that it looked as though one could lift it from its place with one hand. I stood for a long time by the tomb of Canova, and could not take my eyes off the melancholy lion. And in the Palace of the Doges I was always drawn to the corner where the portrait of the unhappy Marino Faliero was painted over with black. "It is fine to be an artist, a poet, a dramatist," I thought, "but since that is not vouchsafed to me, if only I could go in for mysticism! If only I had a grain of some faith to add to the unruffled peace and serenity that fills the soul!"

In the evening we ate oysters, drank wine, and went out in a gondola. I remember our black gondola swayed softly in the same place while the water faintly gurgled under it. Here and there the reflection of the stars and the lights on the bank quivered and trembled. Not far from us in a gondola, hung with coloured lanterns which were reflected in the water, there were people singing. The sounds of guitars, of violins, of mandolins, of men's and women's voices, were audible in the dark. Zinaida Fyodorovna, pale, with a grave, almost stern face, was sitting beside me, compressing her lips and clenching her hands. She was thinking about something; she did not stir an eyelash, nor hear me. Her face, her attitude, and her fixed, expressionless gaze, and her incredibly miserable, dreadful, and icy-cold memories, and around her the gondolas, the lights, the music, the song with its vigorous passionate cry of "Jam-mo! Jam-mo!" -- what contrasts in life! When she sat like that, with tightly clasped hands, stony, mournful, I used to feel as though we were both characters in some novel in the old-fashioned style called "The Ill-fated," "The Abandoned," or something of the sort. Both of us: she -- the ill-fated, the abandoned; and I -- the faithful, devoted friend, the dreamer, and, if you like it, a superfluous man, a failure capable of nothing but coughing and dreaming, and perhaps sacrificing myself.

But who and what needed my sacrifices now? And what had I to sacrifice, indeed?

When we came in in the evening we always drank tea in her room and talked. We did not shrink from touching on old, unhealed wounds -- on the contrary, for some reason I felt a positive pleasure in telling her about my life at Orlov's, or referring openly to relations which I knew and which could not have been concealed from me.

"At moments I hated you," I said to her. "When he was capricious, condescending, told you lies, I marvelled how it was you did not see, did not understand, when it was all so clear! You kissed his hands, you knelt to him, you flattered him. . ."

"When I . . . kissed his hands and knelt to him, I loved him . . ." she said, blushing crimson.

"Can it have been so difficult to see through him? A fine sphinx! A sphinx indeed -- a kammer-junker! I reproach you for nothing, God forbid," I went on, feeling I was coarse, that I had not the tact, the delicacy which are so essential when you have to do with a fellow-creature's soul; in early days before I knew her I had not noticed this defect in myself. "But how could you fail to see what he was," I went on, speaking more softly and more diffidently, however.

"You mean to say you despise my past, and you are right," she said, deeply stirred. " You belong to a special class of men who cannot be judged by ordinary standards; your moral requirements are exceptionally rigorous, and I understand you can't forgive things. I understand you, and if sometimes I say the opposite, it doesn't mean that I look at things differently from you; I speak the same old nonsense simply because I haven't had time yet to wear out my old clothes and prejudices. I, too, hate and despise my past, and Orlov and my love. . . . What was that love? It's positively absurd now," she said, going to the window and looking down at the canal. "All this love only clouds the conscience and confuses the mind. The meaning of life is to be found only in one thing -- fighting. To get one's heel on the vile head of the serpent and to crush it! That's the meaning of life. In that alone or in nothing."

I told her long stories of my past, and described my really astounding adventures. But of the change that had taken place in me I did not say one word. She always listened to me with great attention, and at interesting places she rubbed her hands as though vexed that it had not yet been her lot to experience such adventures, such joys and terrors. Then she would suddenly fall to musing and retreat into herself, and I could see from her face that she was not attending to me.

I closed the windows that looked out on the canal and asked whether we should not have the fire lighted.

"No, never mind. I am not cold," she said, smiling listlessly. "I only feel weak. Do you know, I fancy I have grown much wiser lately. I have extraordinary, original ideas now. When I think of my past, of my life then . . . people in general, in fact, it is all summed up for me in the image of my stepmother. Coarse, insolent, soulless, false, depraved, and a morphia maniac too. My father, who was feeble and weak-willed, married my mother for her money and drove her into consumption; but his second wife, my stepmother, he loved passionately, insanely. . . . What I had to put up with! But what is the use of talking! And so, as I say, it is all summed up in her image. . . . And it vexes me that my stepmother is dead. I should like to meet her now!"

"Why?"

"I don't know," she answered with a laugh and a graceful movement of her head. "Good-night. You must get well. As soon as you are well, we'll take up our work. . . It's time to begin."

After I had said good-night and had my hand on the door-handle, she said:

"What do you think? Is Polya still living there?"

"Probably."

And I went off to my room. So we spent a whole month. One grey morning when we both stood at my window, looking at the clouds which were moving up from the sea, and at the darkening canal, expecting every minute that it would pour with rain, and when a thick, narrow streak of rain covered the sea as though with a muslin veil, we both felt suddenly dreary. The same day we both set off for Florence.

XVI

It was autumn, at Nice. One morning when I went into her room she was sitting on a low chair, bent together and huddled up, with her legs crossed and her face hidden in her hands. She was weeping bitterly, with sobs, and her long, unbrushed hair fell on her knees. The impression of the exquisite marvellous sea which I had only just seen and of which I wanted to tell her, left me all at once, and my heart ached.

"What is it?" I asked; she took one hand from her face and motioned me to go away. "What is it?" I repeated, and for the first time during our acquaintance I kissed her hand.

"No, it's nothing, nothing," she said quickly. "Oh, it's nothing, nothing. . . . Go away. . . . You see, I am not dressed."

I went out overwhelmed. The calm and serene mood in which I had been for so long was poisoned by compassion. I had a passionate longing to fall at her feet, to entreat her not to weep in solitude, but to share her grief with me, and the monotonous murmur of the sea already sounded a gloomy prophecy in my ears, and I foresaw fresh tears, fresh troubles, and fresh losses in the future. "What is she crying about? What is it?" I wondered, recalling her face and her agonised look. I remembered she was with child. She tried to conceal her condition from other people, and also from herself. At home she went about in a loose wrapper or in a blouse with extremely full folds over the bosom, and when she went out anywhere she laced herself in so tightly that on two occasions she fainted when we were out. She never spoke to me of her condition, and when I hinted that it might be as well to see a doctor, she flushed crimson and said not a word.

When I went to see her next time she was already dressed and had her hair done.

"There, there," I said, seeing that she was ready to cry again. "We had better go to the sea and have a talk."

74

"I can't talk. Forgive me, I am in the mood now when one wants to be alone. And, if you please, Vladimir Ivanitch, another time you want to come into my room, be so good as to give a knock at the door."

That "be so good" had a peculiar, unfeminine sound. I went away. My accursed Petersburg mood came back, and all my dreams were crushed and crumpled up like leaves by the heat. I felt I was alone again and there was no nearness between us. I was no more to her than that cobweb to that palm-tree, which hangs on it by chance and which will be torn off and carried away by the wind. I walked about the square where the band was playing, went into the Casino; there I looked at overdressed and heavily perfumed women, and every one of them glanced at me as though she would say: "You are alone; that's all right." Then I went out on the terrace and looked for a long time at the sea. There was not one sail on the horizon. On the left bank, in the lilac-coloured mist, there were mountains, gardens, towers, and houses, the sun was sparkling over it all, but it was all alien, indifferent, an incomprehensible tangle.

XVII

She used as before to come into my room in the morning to coffee, but we no longer dined together, as she said she was not hungry; and she lived only on coffee, tea, and various trifles such as oranges and caramels.

And we no longer had conversations in the evening. I don't know why it was like this. Ever since the day when I had found her in tears she had treated me somehow lightly, at times casually, even ironically, and for some reason called me "My good sir." What had before seemed to her terrible, heroic, marvellous, and had stirred her envy and enthusiasm, did not touch her now at all, and usually after listening to me, she stretched and said:

"Yes, 'great things were done in days of yore,' my good sir."

It sometimes happened even that I did not see her for days together. I would knock timidly and guiltily at her door and get no answer; I would knock again -- still silence. . . . I would stand near the door and listen; then the chambermaid would pass and say coldly, "Madame est partie." Then I would walk about the passages of the hotel, walk and walk. . . . English people, full-bosomed ladies, waiters in swallow-tails. . . . And as I keep gazing at the long striped rug that stretches the whole length of the corridor, the idea occurs to me that I am playing in the life of this woman a strange, probably false part, and that it is beyond my power to alter that part. I run to my room and fall on my bed, and think and think, and can come to no conclusion; and all that is clear to me is that I want to live, and that the plainer and the colder and the harder her face grows, the nearer she is to me, and the more intensely and painfully I feel our kinship. Never mind "My good sir," never mind her light careless tone, never mind anything you like, only don't leave me, my treasure. I am afraid to be alone.

Then I go out into the corridor again, listen in a tremor. . . . I have no dinner; I don't notice the approach of evening. At last about eleven I hear the familiar footstep, and at the turn near the stairs Zinaida Fyodorovna comes into sight.

"Are you taking a walk?" she would ask as she passes me. "You had better go out into the air. . . . Good-night!"

"But shall we not meet again to-day?"

"I think it's late. But as you like."

"Tell me, where have you been?" I would ask, following her into the room.

"Where? To Monte Carlo." She took ten gold coins out of her pocket and said: "Look, my good sir; I have won. That's at roulette."

"Nonsense! As though you would gamble."

"Why not? I am going again to-morrow."

I imagined her with a sick and morbid face, in her condition, tightly laced, standing near the gaming-table in a crowd of cocottes, of old women in their dotage who swarm round the gold like flies round the honey. I remembered she had gone off to Monte Carlo for some reason in secret from me.

"I don't believe you," I said one day. "You wouldn't go there."

"Don't agitate yourself. I can't lose much."

"It's not the question of what you lose," I said with annoyance. "Has it never occurred to you while you were playing there that the glitter of gold, all these women, young and old, the croupiers, all the surroundings -- that it is all a vile, loathsome mockery at the toiler's labour, at his bloody sweat?

"If one doesn't play, what is one to do here?" she asked. "The toiler's labour and his bloody sweat -- all that eloquence you can put off till another time; but now, since you have begun, let me go on. Let me ask you bluntly, what is there for me to do here, and what am I to do?"

"What are you to do?" I said, shrugging my shoulders. "That's a question that can't be answered straight off."

"I beg you to answer me honestly, Vladimir Ivanitch," she said, and her face looked angry. "Once I have brought myself to ask you this question, I am not going to listen to stock phrases. I am asking you," she went on, beating her hand on the table, as though marking time, "what ought I to do here? And not only here at Nice, but in general?"

I did not speak, but looked out of window to the sea. My heart was beating terribly.

"Vladimir Ivanitch," she said softly and breathlessly; it was hard for her to speak -- "Vladimir Ivanitch, if you do not believe in the cause yourself, if you no longer think of going back to it, why . . . why did you drag me out of Petersburg? Why did you make me promises, why did you rouse mad hopes? Your convictions have changed; you have become a different man, and nobody blames you for it -- our convictions are not always in our power. But . . . but, Vladimir Ivanitch, for God's sake, why are you not sincere?" she went on softly, coming up to me. "All these months when I have been dreaming aloud, raving, going into raptures over my plans, remodelling my life on a new pattern, why didn't you tell me the truth? Why were you silent or encouraged me by your stories, and behaved as though you were in complete sympathy with me? Why was it? Why was it necessary?"

"It's difficult to acknowledge one's bankruptcy," I said, turning round, but not looking at her. "Yes, I have no faith; I am worn out. I have lost heart. . . . It is difficult to be truthful -- very difficult, and I held my tongue. God forbid that any one should have to go through what I have been through."

I felt that I was on the point of tears, and ceased speaking.

"Vladimir Ivanitch," she said, and took me by both hands, "you have been through so much and seen so much of life, you know more than I do; think seriously, and tell me, what am I to do? Teach me! If you haven't the strength to go forward yourself and take others with you, at least show me where to go. After all, I am a living, feeling, thinking being. To sink into a false position . . . to play an absurd part . . . is painful to me. I don't reproach you, I don't blame you; I only ask you."

Tea was brought in.

"Well?" said Zinaida Fyodorovna, giving me a glass. "What do you say to me?"

"There is more light in the world than you see through your window," I answered. "And there are other people besides me, Zinaida Fyodorovna."

"Then tell me who they are," she said eagerly. "That's all I ask of you."

"And I want to say, too, I went on, "one can serve an idea in more than one calling. If one has made a mistake and lost faith in one, one may find another. The world of ideas is large and cannot be exhausted."

"The world of ideas!" she said, and she looked into my face sarcastically. "Then we had better leave off talking. What's the use? . . ."

She flushed.

"The world of ideas!" she repeated. She threw her dinner-napkin aside, and an expression of indignation and contempt came into her face. "All your fine ideas, I see, lead up to one inevitable, essential step: I ought to become your mistress. That's what's wanted. To be taken up with ideas without being the mistress of an honourable, progressive man, is as good as not understanding the ideas. One has to begin with that . . . that is, with being your mistress, and the rest will come of itself."

"You are irritated, Zinaida Fyodorovna," I said.

"No, I am sincere!" she cried, breathing hard. "I am sincere!"

"You are sincere, perhaps, but you are in error, and it hurts me to hear you."

"I am in error?" she laughed. "Any one else might say that, but not you, my dear sir! I may seem to you indelicate, cruel, but I don't care: you love me? You love me, don't you?"

I shrugged my shoulders.

"Yes, shrug your shoulders!" she went on sarcastically. "When you were ill I heard you in your delirium, and ever since these adoring eyes, these sighs, and edifying conversations about friendship, about spiritual kinship. . . . But the point is, why haven't you been sincere? Why have you concealed what is and talked about what isn't? Had you said from the beginning what ideas exactly led you to drag me from Petersburg, I should have known. I should have poisoned myself then as I meant to, and there would have been none of this tedious farce. . . . But what's the use of talking!"

79

With a wave of the hand she sat down.

"You speak to me as though you suspected me of dishonourable intentions," I said, offended.

"Oh, very well. What's the use of talking! I don't suspect you of intentions, but of having no intentions. If you had any, I should have known them by now. You had nothing but ideas and love. For the present -- ideas and love, and in prospect -- me as your mistress. That's in the order of things both in life and in novels. . . . Here you abused him," she said, and she slapped the table with her hand, "but one can't help agreeing with him. He has good reasons for despising these ideas."

"He does not despise ideas; he is afraid of them," I cried. "He is a coward and a liar."

"Oh, very well. He is a coward and a liar, and deceived me. And you? Excuse my frankness; what are you? He deceived me and left me to take my chance in Petersburg, and you have deceived me and abandoned me here. But he did not mix up ideas with his deceit, and you . . ."

"For goodness' sake, why are you saying this?" I cried in horror, wringing my hands and going up to her quickly. "No, Zinaida Fyodorovna, this is cynicism. You must not be so despairing; listen to me," I went on, catching at a thought which flashed dimly upon me, and which seemed to me might still save us both. "Listen. I have passed through so many experiences in my time that my head goes round at the thought of them, and I have realised with my mind, with my racked soul, that man finds his true destiny in nothing if not in self-sacrificing love for his neighbour. It is towards that we must strive, and that is our destination! That is my faith!"

I wanted to go on to speak of mercy, of forgiveness, but there was an insincere note in my voice, and I was embarrassed.

"I want to live!" I said genuinely. "To live, to live! I want peace, tranquillity; I want warmth -- this sea here -- to have you near. Oh, how I wish I could rouse in you the same thirst for life! You spoke just now of love, but it would be enough for me to have you near, to hear your voice, to watch the look in your face . . . !"

She flushed crimson, and to hinder my speaking, said quickly:

"You love life, and I hate it. So our ways lie apart."

She poured herself out some tea, but did not touch it, went into the bedroom, and lay down.

"I imagine it is better to cut short this conversation," she said to me from within. "Everything is over for me, and I want nothing. . . . What more is there to say?"

"No, it's not all over!"

"Oh, very well! . . . I know! I am sick of it. . . . That's enough."

I got up, took a turn from one end of the room to the other, and went out into the corridor. When late at night I went to her door and listened, I distinctly heard her crying.

Next morning the waiter, handing me my clothes, informed me, with a smile, that the lady in number thirteen was confined. I dressed somehow, and almost fainting with terror ran to Zinaida Fyodorovna. In her room I found a doctor, a midwife, and an elderly Russian lady from Harkov, called Darya Milhailovna. There was a smell of ether. I had scarcely crossed the threshold when from the room where she was lying I heard a low, plaintive moan, and, as though it had been wafted me by the wind from Russia, I thought of Orlov, his irony, Polya, the Neva, the drifting snow, then the cab without an apron, the prediction I had read in the cold morning sky, and the despairing cry "Nina! Nina!"

"Go in to her," said the lady.

I went in to see Zinaida Fyodorovna, feeling as though I were the father of the child. She was lying with her eyes closed, looking thin and pale, wearing a white cap edged with lace. I remember there were two expressions on her face: one -- cold, indifferent, apathetic;

the other -- a look of childish helplessness given her by the white cap. She did not hear me come in, or heard, perhaps, but did not pay attention. I stood, looked at her, and waited.

But her face was contorted with pain; she opened her eyes and gazed at the ceiling, as though wondering what was happening to her. . . . There was a look of loathing on her face.

"It's horrible . . ." she whispered.

"Zinaida Fyodorovna." I spoke her name softly. She looked at me indifferently, listlessly, and closed her eyes. I stood there a little while, then went away.

At night, Darya Mihailovna informed me that the child, a girl, was born, but that the mother was in a dangerous condition. Then I heard noise and bustle in the passage. Darya Mihailovna came to me again and with a face of despair, wringing her hands, said:

"Oh, this is awful! The doctor suspects that she has taken poison! Oh, how badly Russians do behave here!"

And at twelve o'clock the next day Zinaida Fyodorovna died.

XVIII

Two years had passed. Circumstances had changed; I had come to Petersburg again and could live here openly. I was no longer afraid of being and seeming sentimental, and gave myself up entirely to the fatherly, or rather idolatrous feeling roused in me by Sonya, Zinaida Fyodorovna's child. I fed her with my own hands, gave her her bath, put her to bed, never took my eyes off her for nights together, and screamed when it seemed to me that the nurse was just going to drop her. My thirst for normal ordinary life became stronger and more acute as time went on, but wider visions stopped short at Sonya, as though I had found in her at last just what I needed. I loved the child madly. In her I saw the continuation of my life, and it was not exactly that I fancied, but I felt, I almost believed, that when I had cast off at last my long, bony, bearded frame, I should go on living in those little blue eyes, that silky flaxen hair, those dimpled pink hands which stroked my face so lovingly and were clasped round my neck.

Sonya's future made me anxious. Orlov was her father; in her birth certificate she was called Krasnovsky, and the only person who knew of her existence, and took interest in her -- that is, I -- was at death's door. I had to think about her seriously.

The day after I arrived in Petersburg I went to see Orlov. The door was opened to me by a stout old fellow with red whiskers and no moustache, who looked like a German. Polya, who was tidying the drawing-room, did not recognise me, but Orlov knew me at once.

"Ah, Mr. Revolutionist!" he said, looking at me with curiosity, and laughing. "What fate has brought you?"

He was not changed in the least: the same well-groomed, unpleasant face, the same irony. And a new book was lying on the table just as of old, with an ivory paper-knife thrust in it. He had evidently been reading before I came in. He made me sit down, offered me a cigar, and with a delicacy only found in well-bred people, concealing the unpleasant feeling aroused by my face and my wasted figure, observed casually that I was not in the least changed, and that he would have known me anywhere in spite of my having grown a beard. We talked of the weather, of Paris. To dispose as quickly as possible of the oppressive, inevitable question, which weighed upon him and me, he asked:

"Zinaida Fyodorovna is dead?"

"Yes," I answered.

"In childbirth?"

"Yes, in childbirth. The doctor suspected another cause of death, but . . . it is more comforting for you and for me to think that she died in childbirth."

83

He sighed decorously and was silent. The angel of silence passed over us, as they say.

"Yes. And here everything is as it used to be -- no changes," he said briskly, seeing that I was looking about the room. "My father, as you know, has left the service and is living in retirement; I am still in the same department. Do you remember Pekarsky? He is just the same as ever. Gruzin died of diphtheria a year ago. . . . Kukushkin is alive, and often speaks of you. By the way," said Orlov, dropping his eyes with an air of reserve, "when Kukushkin heard who you were, he began telling every one you had attacked him and tried to murder him . . . and that he only just escaped with his life."

I did not speak.

"Old servants do not forget their masters. . . . It's very nice of you," said Orlov jocosely. "Will you have some wine and some coffee, though? I will tell them to make some."

"No, thank you. I have come to see you about a very important matter, Georgy Ivanitch."

"I am not very fond of important matters, but I shall be glad to be of service to you. What do you want?"

"You see," I began, growing agitated, "I have here with me Zinaida Fyodorovna's daughter. . . . Hitherto I have brought her up, but, as you see, before many days I shall be an empty sound. I should like to die with the thought that she is provided for."

Orlov coloured a little, frowned a little, and took a cursory and sullen glance at me. He was unpleasantly affected, not so much by the "important matter" as by my words about death, about becoming an empty sound.

"Yes, it must be thought about," he said, screening his eyes as though from the sun. "Thank you. You say it's a girl?"

"Yes, a girl. A wonderful child!"

84

"Yes. Of course, it's not a lap-dog, but a human being. I understand we must consider it seriously. I am prepared to do my part, and am very grateful to you."

He got up, walked about, biting his nails, and stopped before a picture.

"We must think about it," he said in a hollow voice, standing with his back to me. "I shall go to Pekarsky's to-day and will ask him to go to Krasnovsky's. I don't think he will make much ado about consenting to take the child."

"But, excuse me, I don't see what Krasnovsky has got to do with it," I said, also getting up and walking to a picture at the other end of the room.

"But she bears his name, of course!" said Orlov.

"Yes, he may be legally obliged to accept the child -- I don't know; but I came to you, Georgy Ivanitch, not to discuss the legal aspect."

"Yes, yes, you are right," he agreed briskly. "I believe I am talking nonsense. But don't excite yourself. We will decide the matter to our mutual satisfaction. If one thing won't do, we'll try another; and if that won't do, we'll try a third -- one way or another this delicate question shall be settled. Pekarsky will arrange it all. Be so good as to leave me your address and I will let you know at once what we decide. Where are you living?"

Orlov wrote down my address, sighed, and said with a smile:

"Oh, Lord, what a job it is to be the father of a little daughter! But Pekarsky will arrange it all. He is a sensible man. Did you stay long in Paris?"

"Two months."

We were silent. Orlov was evidently afraid I should begin talking of the child again, and to turn my attention in another direction, said:

"You have probably forgotten your letter by now. But I have kept it. I understand your mood at the time, and, I must own, I respect that letter. 'Damnable cold blood,' 'Asiatic,' 'coarse laugh' -- that was charming and characteristic," he went on with an ironical smile. "And the fundamental thought is perhaps near the truth, though one might dispute the question endlessly. That is," he hesitated, "not dispute the thought itself, but your attitude to the question -- your temperament, so to say. Yes, my life is abnormal, corrupted, of no use to any one, and what prevents me from beginning a new life is cowardice -- there you are quite right. But that you take it so much to heart, are troubled, and reduced to despair by it -- that's irrational; there you are quite wrong."

"A living man cannot help being troubled and reduced to despair when he sees that he himself is going to ruin and others are going to ruin round him."

"Who doubts it! I am not advocating indifference; all I ask for is an objective attitude to life. The more objective, the less danger of falling into error. One must look into the root of things, and try to see in every phenomenon a cause of all the other causes. We have grown feeble, slack -- degraded, in fact. Our generation is entirely composed of neurasthenics and whimperers; we do nothing but talk of fatigue and exhaustion. But the fault is neither yours nor mine; we are of too little consequence to affect the destiny of a whole generation. We must suppose for that larger, more general causes with a solid raison d'être from the biological point of view. We are neurasthenics, flabby, renegades, but perhaps it's necessary and of service for generations that will come after us. Not one hair falls from the head without the will of the Heavenly Father -- in other words, nothing happens by chance in Nature and in human environment. Everything has its cause and is inevitable. And if so, why should we worry and write despairing letters?"

"That's all very well," I said, thinking a little. "I believe it will be easier and clearer for the generations to come; our experience will be at their service. But one wants to live apart from future generations and not only for their sake. Life is only given us once, and one wants to live it boldly, with full consciousness and beauty. One wants to play a striking, independent, noble part; one wants to make history so that those generations may not have the right to say of each of us that we were nonentities or worse. . . . I believe what is going on about us is inevitable and not without a purpose, but what have I to do with that inevitability? Why should my ego be lost?"

"Well, there's no help for it," sighed Orlov, getting up and, as it were, giving me to understand that our conversation was over.

I took my hat.

"We've only been sitting here half an hour, and how many questions we have settled, when you come to think of it!" said Orlov, seeing me into the hall. "So I will see to that matter. . . . I will see Pekarsky to-day. . . . Don't be uneasy."

He stood waiting while I put on my coat, and was obviously relieved at the feeling that I was going away.

"Georgy Ivanitch, give me back my letter," I said.

"Certainly."

He went to his study, and a minute later returned with the letter. I thanked him and went away.

The next day I got a letter from him. He congratulated me on the satisfactory settlement of the question. Pekarsky knew a lady, he wrote, who kept a school, something like a kindergarten, where she took quite little children. The lady could be entirely depended upon, but before concluding anything with her it would be as well to discuss the matter with Krasnovsky -- it was a matter of form. He advised me to see Pekarsky at once and to take the birth certificate with me, if I had it. "Rest assured of the sincere respect and devotion of your humble servant. . . ."

I read this letter, and Sonya sat on the table and gazed at me attentively without blinking, as though she knew her fate was being decided.

CPSIA information can be obtained
at www.ICGtesting.com
Printed in the USA
LVOW01s0906111216
516771LV00036B/1062/P

9 781503 192843